Stuck at Sundown

Emilia Abraham

Chapter One

Cole

IT had been over ten years since Cole stepped foot into the offices of Waterson & Avery. Harold Waterson never got around to changing the name after Lyle Avery died almost two decades earlier. The town of Sun Oak wasn't big enough to warrant a law office, but Harold did a little of everything to keep it going. With several ranches in the area, he kept plugging along, well into his 70s.

Not much had changed since Cole last visited with his great-aunt Muriel. Harold led him into the same office, with the same worn carpet and uncomfortable wooden chairs. At 17, Cole was shell-shocked. At 30, he knew what to expect, making it easier to swallow being there.

"I sure am sorry I didn't get to see Muriel more since she

moved off to the city," Harold said, settling himself into his creaky, leather chair. "Once she made up her mind there was no changing her plan."

"That's for sure," Cole agreed. "Nothing I could do to convince her to stay on when she made her decision to leave."

"I hear the ranch is doing well. Almost calving season, isn't it?" Harold shuffled around some papers, glancing between the door and clock.

"It is. Should be a good year with the price of beef nowadays." Cole despised small talk, but there was no rushing Harold. He'd get on with it in his own time.

"Well, I guess we should get started," he said pulling out a packet.

"There are some specific things lined out by Muriel in the will, like not having a funeral. Another was a proper reading. Commonly, people don't do this anymore, but she said it was a damn shame since it was a good start of a story. At any rate, this is the reading of the will of Muriel Ann Pierson, dated May..." Harold stopped talking at a sudden commotion at the door.

"So sorry I'm late! I followed the GPS and it kept redirecting and I got turned around." A woman in her late 20s dashed through the door and dropped down next to Cole. Her chestnut hair, pulled into a ponytail, swung back and forth announcing her entrance. She plopped her purse down and glanced his way, allowing him to catch a hint of brown eyes before she turned back to Harold.

"Ahh, Miss Summers I presume? Glad you could make it. Don't worry about it. We were about to get started. Cole, this is Abigail Summers. She was Muriel's neighbor and friend in the city. Miss Summers, this is Cole Pierson, Muriel's great-nephew." Harold smiled widely at the pair of them, as Cole continued to stare at the tornado of a woman.

"Oh, call me Abby," she smiled as she twisted around to face Cole, "I've heard so much about you! Muriel talked about you all the time. It's good to finally meet." She held out her hand but Cole ignored it, dumbstruck.

How does she know who I am, but I have no clue who she is?

Awkwardly she withdrew her hand. A buzzing filled his ears, drowning them out while they resumed their conversation. Muriel never mentioned a neighbor. Whenever Cole visited, she made it sound like she was all alone. At the time, he'd felt guilty, but if she had this friend, why not bring it up? Why not introduce them? The woman's voice cut through his thoughts.

"I'm sorry Mr. Waterson. Muriel was my friend, but she never said I'd be in her will, so I'm a little confused why I'm here."

You and me both lady.

Harold nodded and cleared his throat, "well, yes. She held you in high regard, Miss Summers. As to why you're here, some specifics involve you. Muriel wanted you to know how much your friendship meant to her over these past few years."

Cole watched her head dip and her lips pressed into a thin line. He hoped she didn't start crying. The last thing he, or Harold for that matter, would be able to handle was a sobbing woman neither of them knew.

The lawyer coughed, "okay, let's continue. As you know, there is the house in the city, the possessions within, and the Sundown Ranch, as well as a sum of money in an estate account. The house in the city is to be repaired and, along with her possessions therein, sold. There are a few items named to you, Miss Summers. I have a list here. The profit from the sale will be added to the estate account. An executor has been named through an agency to take care of those things. The remaining balance in the estate account will be transferred into your name Cole."

Harold paused, the look on his face making Cole's muscles bunch, but he forced himself to relax. Muriel wouldn't have thrown any surprises into her will. Cole knew this reading was a formality, one last crazy antic of a woman who did what she wanted, with little regard to what others thought. She told him long ago he would inherit Sundown

Ranch. She'd never mentioned Abigail Summers, but if they were friends, it made sense Muriel would leave her some knick-knack or tea set. It solved the mystery of this woman at least.

"Muriel wrote each of you a letter. I haven't read them. She asked me to tell you to open them after you left the office, whenever you were ready." He handed over an envelope to each of them. Cole left it on the edge of the desk, while Miss Summers, Abigail, clutched hers like a lifeline.

"With regard to the ranch…" he trailed off, sucking in a deep breath and pulling at his tie, "this might come as a surprise, but Muriel split the ranch 50/50 between you two."

Silence filled the office. He must have heard wrong. This had to be a joke. One last lark from Muriel before she was put in the ground. Muriel wouldn't demolish his legacy without giving him a heads up. This couldn't be happening.

"Excuse me?" Cole asked sharply, causing Harold to wince, "Harold, you can't be serious." The lawyer's mouth opened and snapped shut, searching for some way to explain this bizarre scenario.

"I know it's a little unprecedented Cole, but Muriel was set in how she wanted to divide things."

"Unprecedented? This is insane is what it is!" he sputtered.

How could Muriel do this to him? Sundown was his home since birth. He was the reason it was still running, still making money, still in the family, and now he would be forced to share it? Absolutely not.

"Again, I understand this is a shock to you both." Harold held his hands up, trying to placate him. "I assure you, Muriel knew what she was doing."

"But I've never heard of this woman before!" Cole exploded, jumping to his feet and gesturing wildly at her. His eyes flashed to Abigail, who sat stunned. Her blank eyes were fixed on the wall behind Harold.

"Cole, please, sit down. Muriel was quite clear this was not a reflection of you or the running of Sundown. I tried to get an explanation, but she wouldn't budge, but there are some conditions. Please, let's get through this."

Cole didn't care about the conditions, but he sat. He could see his legacy slipping away at the hands of this woman. Still frozen in her seat, Abigail hadn't reacted to his outburst.

"Now, this 50/50 split will only happen if you both agree. If either of you decides to rescind your half of the ranch, neither will receive any portion of it. The spread, along with all other assets will go up for auction and you both will be banned from participating in said auction. The proceeds of the sale, herein, will be donated to a charity specified in the document. If anyone contests the will, all the assets previously stated will be liquidated and the proceeds will be donated to the same charity."

Cole felt like his lungs were trying to shrivel up. Only one question reverberated through his head.

Why?

He glanced at the woman next to him, trying to glean any insight, but her face was still blank. Either she had no idea this was coming, or she was a very good actress. Muriel didn't do anything halfway, so it was much more likely Abigail knew before today. Maybe she didn't think Muriel would go through with it.

"What are the conditions," Abigail asked after a beat.

"Ah, an excellent question, m'dear!" Harold shot her a relieved look.

"So, beginning the following month after Muriel's passing, Miss Summers, you are required to move to the ranch for a period of no less than six months. You must live on the ranch for the entirety of the six months. Cole, you are to provide housing on the property to Miss Summers for the duration of her stay. After six months, you are free to leave the ranch, either selling to the other upon your departure or retaining your half of the shares. Should one of you choose to sell to the other, the price shall be based on the assessment value at the time the will was dated."

"We have to live on the ranch, for six months, and then she can sell me her portion? Is that what you're saying?" He'd waited this long to officially own the ranch, six more months would be nothing, but having to live with a stranger? Who would legally hold half of it? She didn't look like she'd ever been on a ranch, much less be able to live on one.

"Should you both choose to retain your half of the ranch at the end of six months, you will run it jointly, but either of you would be free to pursue lodging elsewhere," Harold said.

Silence filled the room again, both lost in thought as Harold's gaze bounced between them. Abigail gazed at the envelope containing her letter from Muriel, still gripped tightly in her hands. Cole was still having a battle with his lungs. He didn't know if he could speak past the lump in his throat. That one word was still bouncing around in his skull.

Why? Why? Why?

Muriel was a no-nonsense woman. Cole never knew her to be convoluted about anything, much less something as serious as this. The ranch had been her world. Before Uncle Harlan died, she lived and breathed the land. She held things together with Cole's dad and uncle after he'd passed. Why would she do something so asinine? What had this woman filled her head with since she moved next door to Muriel to convince his aunt she deserved anything, much less his legacy? His birthright?

Cole took in a deep breath, "why."

"I don't know Cole. She was quite adamant this needed to be the terms. I'm sure her letter will shed some insight into what she was thinking at the time."

Harold waited as if Cole would start throwing things next. He wanted to, but he wouldn't. The more he sat there thinking, the more he was convinced this woman was a con artist. Somehow, she convinced Muriel to give her half of the ranch. Sundown was now in jeopardy, and he couldn't even contest the will. He couldn't threaten her not to come, or he would be edged out of the only place he'd called home; the only place he ever belonged.

Bolting up he snatched the letter off the desk with a grunt. He couldn't sit here any longer, waiting for answers Harold didn't have. Cole stalked from the room, straight towards his truck without a backward glance. There must be a way out of this mess. There was no way he would let someone waltz in and take what he'd worked so hard for. Once inside the cab, he could see Harold through his windshield, speaking with Abigail in the lobby. He watched, seething, as Harold handed her a business card and patted her shoulder, as if she was the one in need of comfort.

She walked out of the office to a beat-up sedan. No wonder she wanted the ranch. She was likely broke and needed the cash. Muriel must have looked like an easy mark to her. Cole watched as she climbed in and pulled her door shut once, and again when the door didn't latch properly. He could see as she opened the letter from Muriel and read it through. What did it say? Probably more of how she'd be taken care of now that Muriel gave half the family ranch to her. She'd never have to worry again.

Then the back of her head bowed and her shoulders shook, laughing at how things turned out, but as he heard a broken sob make its way out her open window, he paused. Could she be as much of a victim of Muriel's sudden scheming as he was?

When he started his truck and pulled away though, he knew it was for Harold's benefit, if not his own. Her acting was decent, but she wouldn't fool him. He'd find out how she'd tricked Muriel, and he'd kick her ass out when those six months were up. Nothing would stand in the way of preserving the Pierson legacy. Especially not Abigail Summers.

Chapter Two

Abby

ABBY drove in a daze after leaving the lawyer's office, scarcely registering the ride into the city. By the time she pulled in front of her bungalow, it was early afternoon. Muriel's gray craftsman sat ten feet away, a white fence dividing the two properties. Abby could picture Muriel stepping out her door, ridiculous teacup in hand, waiting for Abby to tell her about her day.

But the door stayed shut. No cheery glow lit up the windows lining the blue door. No teacup shaped like a cow resting on the table, flanking the rocking chairs on the porch. No Muriel. After all the stress from today, Abby couldn't handle going in to box up more of Muriel's belongings. With an executor set to do the work, she didn't know if she should anyways. Some stranger was to handle Muriel's possessions.

Abby pulled out the paper listing the things Muriel had willed to her. There weren't many, only seven items, but each one pulled a little more at her heart. These were things special to her, because of the memories they dredged up. The tea set they always used together. The embroidered pillow Abby gifted Muriel on her birthday two years prior. The Afghan blanket they used on cooler nights while rocking. No one else would want these things. The list became hazy and tears fell from her eyes.

The shock from the reading of Muriel's will was wearing off now. She understood the reaction Muriel's nephew had wasn't about her, not really. Abby wasn't thrilled to be shoved into this awkward situation any more than he was, but after reading Muriel's letter, she understood. Her friend always had something tucked away-another scheme, another adventure, another prank. Now the shock had worn off, it made perfect sense Muriel would come up with this elaborate plan. She never did anything halfway. Now Abby had to make a decision on to stay where she was, or take what Muriel was dangling in front of her. No matter how much Muriel thought she knew better than everyone else around her, she always let Abby make her own choices in the end.

Trying to figure out what she wanted to do after the long day was impossible. She stuffed the paper away and hurried in her house. She'd think about everything tomorrow after she slept off the shock that Muriel had much more in store for her than a few trinkets to remember her by.

Abby's alarm clock jarred her out of a restless sleep. The pain of losing Muriel still fresh, and she'd spent the night replaying memories of their time together and those lead to remembering the events at the lawyer's office and then the letter, and she'd fall apart all over again.

It was kismet when she bought the house next to Muriel, less than a year after her parents' accident. It was as if fate intervened and said, 'here! This is where you're meant to be. Now heal.' Muriel turned out to be the balm that soothed the jagged wounds of losing them. She hadn't told the older woman anything at first, but Muriel sensed she was aching. She demanded Abby come over for tea, even though Abby didn't drink tea at the time. Over the last five years, Muriel converted her.

Muriel became Abby's saving grace, and now that she was gone, Abby felt adrift once more. How would she cope, losing her lifeline? How could she wake up and trudge to her job, day after day, knowing no one was waiting for her when she got home?

Muriel often lamented Abby was destined for something more than her drone-like desk job. It gave her something to do five days a week and paid the bills, but that was it. After her parents passed, she switched to auto pilot. She'd changed majors, graduated early, and took the first job that came along. It didn't matter where it was or that she found no joy in it. It was a routine and that was what Abby needed at the time.

Muriel pushed her for years to find something else. Something that would excite her; that would help her live. Now that Muriel was gone, Abby hardly had the energy to go to work, much less pursue something new. Muriel was trying to force her into action, but Abby didn't know if she could find that spark. Her mind drifted back to the letter. Muriel's voice came alive through her words and told her, again, to go live. She needed to stop existing and truly feel something- anything. It was time to stop living in the routine and find passion. Apparently, Muriel thought she could do that at Sundown Ranch.

The glaring issue was wrapped up in the broody rancher who owned the other half. As if his brawny frame wasn't enough, his intimidating presence had filled the small office, even before he started bellowing. Obviously, he hadn't been informed she was going to be there. He didn't seem to know she existed before she burst in like a tornado. Muriel and Abby spent almost every evening together for five years. Surely, Abby came up in their conversations at least once. It was clear she hadn't after he stared at her like she was an intruder on his private meeting with Harold.

Abby knew about him though. Cole Pierson, the acting owner of Sundown, raised on the ranch by his dad, uncle, and Muriel since he was a baby. A godsend to Muriel and a cattle rancher extraordinaire. Muriel sung his praises whenever the ranch was mentioned. According to her, he saved the family legacy time and time again.

As far as Abby knew, he'd only visited a handful of times over the last decade when Muriel moved to the city. With Muriel's recent scheme, it must have been by design they never crossed paths. Looking back, it was a little too coincidental Cole never visited when Abby was around.

Why would Muriel not want them to meet, only to throw them together at Sundown after her death? She'd hoped the letter would shed some light on her friend's decision. Instead, it centered on Abby finding her way. Abby didn't know anything about ranch life, other than what she'd picked up from Muriel. Abby visited a farm when she was eight for school, but she didn't think that counted.

Co-owners. Muriel handed Abby half of her legacy, if only for a short time. No wonder Cole was upset. He'd arrived at Waterson & Avery thinking it was a formality and walked out with a new business partner he'd never met, didn't know, and clearly didn't want.

Abby dragged herself out of bed and into the shower.

Even though it was Sunday, she knew the day would be anything but relaxing. She needed to find the things Muriel left her and figure out what her next step was. She didn't want Cole to lose the ranch, even if he seemed like a grouch. She tried to remind herself as hard as yesterday had been on her, it must have been harder on him. Muriel entrusted him with their heritage, he must have some redeeming qualities. The stress of the day must have hit him hard and that was the reason he acted so outrageously.

After breakfast, Abby tucked her feet into her shoes and grabbed the spare key to the house next door, along with her papers from the lawyer. As she made her way up the porch steps of Muriel's house the door swung open and a man in a black suit stepped out.

"Can I help you?" he asked.

Abby tipped her head up to see him. It was alarming how he towered over her. His shock of gray hair should have softened his features, but it only made him more threatening.

"Hello, I'm Abby. I'm here to collect some things, and you are?" It was hard to be assertive with him still blocking the stairway and glaring at her. She certainly wasn't going to give him her full name or say she lived next door. The man pulled a phone from his pocket, tapping the screen aggressively.

"Abigail Summers?" He peered at her with eyebrows

raised.

"Um, yes?"

He deflated rapidly, anxiety seeping out of him. "I'm sorry Miss Summers. I'm the executor of Ms. Pierson's estate, Marcus Trumbley." He dug into his breast pocket and handed her a business card.

"I spoke with Mr. Pierson earlier, and he was concerned with…strangers trying to gain access to the house. Frankly, I thought he was being paranoid about the city, but then you showed up, looking as if you were going to waltz right in."

"Well, I was going to waltz in, after I used this," she countered holding up her key.

"Ahh, of course." He shot her an embarrassed smile. Had Cole tried to prevent her from going into Muriel's place? She wasn't going to take anything. The way Mr. Trumbley paused, she had the nagging suspicion Cole was afraid she'd steal *his* possessions. Maybe it wasn't just the stress of Muriel's will getting to him. Maybe he was just an asshole.

"Let's go inside and I can explain how this process will go," the man said, ushering her through the door.

It was just as Abby left it on Friday. Scattered around were carefully packed boxes, half-filled with knick knacks, dishes, and books. Abby hadn't touched the pictures lining the walls. Good thing, since Cole might have called the police on her.

"I appreciate you wanting to get a jump on things, but that won't be necessary going forward," Mr. Trumbley said from the living room, "we'll box up the personal items for Mr. Pierson and send them along. Everything else will be donated. Since you're right next door, I assumed you would take your things, but if you'd rather we ship them to the ranch we can."

Ship them? To the ranch? Abby couldn't understand why she would want to ship anything when her house was literal feet away. Confusion must have been apparent on her face, because Mr. Trumbley turned pink and started to stutter.

"Unless you're not moving to the ranch, of course. I assumed you would be going along with the 50/50 split. Of course, you can gather what Ms. Pierson left you and do whatever you like with them," he tapered off into silence.

"Oh, I'll take them with me. I don't see why you would ship something only an hour away," Abby murmured.

She hadn't decided what to do about leaving. Even though it was only for six months, she'd have to quit her job or take a leave of absence at least. Someone would have to keep up with maintenance on her house. She could rent it out, but that was more hassle than she was willing to deal with. It wasn't like anything else was keeping her here, but going off to live with a man she had only heard of, living on a ranch, which she knew nothing about? It seemed insane, but

Muriel had planted the seed of something more in her brain.

The executor nodded his head, not looking at her. Abby wondered if Muriel knew him. He could have been a friend or acquaintance. Was he feeling the presence Abby felt in this room or did he just feel awkward to be standing here, dealing with this strange situation?

"Well, I'll get out of your way. Again, only concern yourself the possessions on your list. We'll take care of that. Take all the time you need, but please lock up when you leave. I'll be back later this week." He made his way into the hallway and out the door before she could respond. It clicked shut, and she was alone, surrounded by only memories and boxes.

Abby wandered around listlessly, gazing at the pictures hanging in the hall, each one the ranch capturing snapshots of a different time. A young Muriel and her husband leaning on a fence. A sunset picture of a large two-story ranch house with a wraparound porch. A boy, no older than seven, riding a horse while an older man lead them around a pen. That must be Cole as a child with his father, with a big, grinning face-joy radiating from him. The pride on the older man's face was evident. She wondered if that grin made an appearance now, 20 years later. Not likely. Cole seemed like the kind of man who was stoic and quiet most of the time, but what did she know. One tense meeting where he didn't speak to her was hardly much of a judgment to go by.

Abby continued on to Muriel's bedroom, pushing the door open and peering inside. She rarely went back here. Muriel's reading glasses still sat on her nightstand, a book sitting next to them with a bookmark sticking out. The pain hit Abby, and she collapsed right there in the hall. She pulled out the letter again and scanned Muriel's steady handwriting through the tears.

Don't be afraid.

Don't hold back.

Find passion.

Live.

With a shaking hand, she pulled out her phone and the card the lawyer gave her. The number written on the back taunted her as Muriel's words echoed through the air. Trembling, she made her decision. Abby sat for a long time, agonizing over a future that no longer included her friend.

Chapter Three

Cole

I'VE decided to stay at the ranch. Be there May 1ˢᵗ.

Cole stared at the text from an unknown number. Unfortunately, he knew who it was from. He'd been awake for three hours, doing chores, but he assumed a woman like her slept in on weekends, but it was only 8:15.

As Cole made himself coffee in the kitchen, relief warred with irritation. Thank god he didn't have to convince her to claim her half, but he didn't know if he could share a house with a stranger for six months. He didn't want to lose his home, but having another person in his space wasn't something he thought he'd have to get used to again.

He thought about putting her up in the cottage by the creek, but couldn't bear to let her live there. He would go there himself instead, if it came to that, but the inconvenience of moving his entire existence there for half a year was enough for him to dismiss the idea for now.

He picked up his phone and read the two lines. Who did she think she was, dictating when she was going to uproot his life? A scammer, that's who. He pushed away the reminder that the will made those decisions for her. Cole knew he wasn't being fair, but the fear of losing everything he worked so hard for overshadowed all else.

Growling, he threw his phone on the counter and grabbed his cup, looking out of the window above the sink. The view was peaceful, unlike the thoughts rolling around his head. Muriel really had put him in the shit this time. Normally, she let him run the ranch how he saw fit, trusting him to do what was right. She never questioned his decisions or loyalty. What changed? Surely, she would have consulted him if she thought about doing something so drastic. Muriel hadn't visited in over a decade, but he kept her up-to-date on everything. She never completely left; she would always be part of the ranch. This place had been in her soul, and she passed that on to him.

Now, with Muriel's antics and that woman's scheming, he might have to leave everything he'd built behind. He didn't want to find out what it would be like to live somewhere other than the ranch. Cole knew he had to stay strong. The possibility of leaving it all behind wasn't an option. He couldn't go to another ranch and work for someone else. Owning a ranch, being the boss, was the only thing he'd known for a long time, and he wouldn't give that up without a fight. Exhaling heavily, Cole dumped the rest of his coffee. Anxiety twisted in his stomach.

What would it be like to have someone else filling this space?

He'd lived alone for a long time. Gazing around the house he grew up in, everything was the way he wanted it, though little had changed from when he was a kid. The furniture was arranged with the same overstuffed couches and tables with the same lamps. The large kitchen island sported a new countertop, but the same stools were tucked underneath. Uncle Harlan used to hang lights from the large picture window at Christmas in the open dining room off the kitchen. When they would gather around the large table, Muriel would add more and more leaves to the table as she roped in the ranch hands who didn't have anywhere else to go. He missed those days; missed Muriel.

Sighing again, Cole made his way through the kitchen to his office, sinking into his desk chair. He peered out the large window at the fields that went on forever. He liked his own company, but even he could admit it got lonely out here once all the workers left. There were only a few on the ranch today, taking care of the horses and checking on the cattle.

Cole had fed the chickens and checked on the heifers who were going to calve soon. He could hear the goats bleating in their pen. He'd herded them back in twice today. Sneaky little shits were always finding their way out to places they weren't supposed to be.

Cole needed to get going on paperwork, but his eyes kept drifting to the papers from the lawyer. Harold had stopped by in the evening, dropping off everything Cole left when he stomped out like a petulant child. He apologized to Harold, but the old man brushed him off; said he knew how Cole would react. That didn't make him feel better.

The envelope from Muriel caught his eye. He couldn't bring himself to read it. He didn't want to know her asinine reasons behind bringing that sham of a woman into this. Muriel knew he was as dedicated to this place as her and Uncle Harlan had been. They wanted the same thing-for the ranch to live on. Cole couldn't imagine Muriel thinking he'd need help. It was clear Abigail didn't know how to run a ranch. She'd be useless at best, a liability at worst.

Cole needed to tell Diego. He was probably going to run into her at some point while she was staying here. He strode out of the house, finding his foreman in the barn, feeding the horses. Trigger, his own horse wouldn't let anyone close, so Cole grabbed the bag and got to work. They worked in silence for several minutes until Diego pulled his gloves off, and turned to him.

"Hey boss, we're running low on feed. Any idea if Adam has some more to get us through before the shipment comes in?" Diego asked. Cole's mind was still on the text from Abigail and it took him a minute to figure out his foreman was talking to him.

"There's more in the auxiliary barn," Cole replied.

"All gone. I already checked."

"Yeah, check there," Cole said, glancing around and trying to remember why he had come here.

"You okay boss?" Diego eyed Cole, narrowing his dark eyes in concern.

"What? Oh, yeah. I'm fine. Listen, we got a thing happening." He tucked his chin to his chest, blowing out a deep breath.

"Okay, what's that?"

"Someone is going to come stay with us until end of October. I'll need you to keep an eye out for her," Cole stated, eyebrows pulled low.

"We going to get her set up as a newbie? Or are you thinking something else?"

"Shit no. I'm sure she's never been on a ranch before. She's from the city," Cole grumbled.

"Well, this'll be interesting. How'd we swing that boss?" Diego's eyebrows disappeared under his dark hair.

"Muriel…" Cole blew out a deep breath, "apparently this woman lived next to her and Muriel thought it would be great to have her live here for six months." Cole wasn't about to tell Diego she owned half of the ranch for that time. It was hard enough dealing with the twist of fate Muriel thrust at him, but telling everyone else is not something he wanted to do. He would lock her in the house if he thought he could get away with it.

"Okay boss. I'm sure it'll be fine. We'll find something for her to do while she's here," Diego reassured him, clapping him on the shoulder as they both gazed out on the field, filled with cattle.

"Just keep an eye on her. Not sure why she's choosing to come here of all places," Cole sighed, frustration bleeding into his voice.

"You said Muriel did it, right? I mean, sounds like she didn't have a choice in the matter."

"She doesn't get anything out of this other than money," he muttered.

Diego's eyebrows disappeared again, but stayed quiet. The horses nickered, drawing Cole's eyes. The phone call with the executor didn't go like he'd planned. He was informed there was nothing they could do to keep her entering Muriel's house. Did he actually think she'd take anything? No, but he was already so turned around by the whole situation, he couldn't figure out which way was up, and he wouldn't be robbed at the same time.

"What does she do in the city then? Seems weird she'd be able to just take off for six months," Diego interrupted Cole's thoughts.

"Something with computers. I don't know. Harold said she lives alone, no ties other than Muriel apparently, but there wasn't much he knew. Muriel was pretty tight-lipped about the whole friendship she was hiding from everyone." Bitterness bled into his words, but he couldn't worry about it. He trusted Diego to not run his mouth around town.

"She single?"

Cole swung his eyes to his foreman, glaring, "yes, why?"

"No reason. I'm sure it'll be great boss. Maybe it'll be good for you."

Cole shook his head and scoffed, "no chance. This is a disaster. She'll come in here, muck everything up, take her money and hopefully run back to the city."

"Hopefully? You think she's out for something else?"

"No idea, but I was blindsided once by this whole thing, I won't be bamboozled too. The only explanation is she got in Muriel's head. I'm not going to let her take Sundown. Don't worry, Diego. I'll figure things out. We'll be just fine."

"Take Sundown?"

"Not going to happen. I told you, I've got a plan," Cole

reassured him before stomping back to the house. He needed to perfect the plan to make her not want to stay after her time was up. Abigail Summers crushed all the dreams of finally being sole owner. Now he had to figure out how to coexist with her, all while convincing her to sell her shares to him. It would be a tightrope walk, but he was sure he could do it, and wave as she drove away on October 31st. There was no way he'd usher in November with her still on his land. He might have to put up with her, but he'd make her wish she'd never connived her way into Sundown Ranch.

Chapter Four

Abby

EVERYTHING was dusty. Abby didn't know what she expected, but it wasn't this much grit. Her old beater car was covered in a fine sheen as she bumped her way up a long, gravel driveway while stalks of wheat waved her on in the breeze.

It took much longer than the hour it was supposed to because she got lost twice on the country roads which weren't marked, and because her car was old-extremely old. She didn't care, as she often took the train to work, but she might have to see about a new one if she was going to be here until the end of October. A brown car, so it would blend in.

She rolled around one last bend and everything opened

up. The sky seemed bigger here, touching the rolling hills of green fields. A large two-story ranch house was nestled into the picturesque view, windows reflecting the sun, and a wraparound porch extended around the back. Dark wood contrasted with the bright red steel roof, matching the front door.

There was only one picture in Muriel's place of this house, the one from Harlan and Muriel's wedding day, but the picture couldn't capture the beauty in what they built together. Off to the right, in the distance were barns and fences for miles, but Abby's eyes were drawn back to the house.

Inching along, still gazing up, a loud bleat rang out near her driver's window. Startled, Abby's foot slammed on the gas and the sound of a gunshot echoed from her tailpipe. She yelped, slammed on the brakes and her car puttered out, leaving a puff of smoke in its wake. Heart racing, Abby whipped her head around and saw…nothing. There was nothing there, nothing on the porch, nothing at all.

Putting the car in park, she got out warily and was surrounded by hooves. Lots of hooves actually-all straight up in the air. Two dozen goats were frozen, scattered around her car. She thought she might be sick.

Five minutes in and she killed Cole's goats. Her shitty, piece of crap car she didn't like all that much, took them out in one fell swoop. Now she'd have to buy him new goats. Aghast with herself for only thinking about the money to buy new goats, she hadn't even considered Cole would be attached to them. Did they have names? Did they have calves? Children? Kids? She didn't even know what baby goats were called, much less if these had any.

Abby approached one and reached out hesitantly. Maybe it was only startled. Some animals played dead, didn't they? Possums or Opossums-she could never figure out the difference-played dead right? Bent over, she went to shake the lifeless goat who might be faking at being dead.

"What the hell did you do to my goats?!"

Abby froze.

Uh oh.

At the sound of Cole's bellow behind her, the goats popped up and started bleating again. Abby bounced back, almost tripping over one. What the hell was this place? Who had goats just wandering around to ambush unsuspecting victims with their shenanigans? Abby spun around to face Cole. The muscles along his arms flexed every time he clenched his fists, a thunderous look in his blue eyes pinned her into place as his dark hair waved slightly in the breeze. Abby knew she was gaping at him, but she hadn't noticed at the lawyers how much taller he was than her. Even across the yard, she could tell he would tower over her.

"Holy shit you're tall," she said under her breath.

"What?" he demanded, but she clamped her mouth shut, refusing to repeat herself.

Clearing her throat of the dust, she started toward him. This was not the impression she was hoping to make when she saw him again. His eyes followed her as she weaved around the animals still meandering about the front yard.

"Did you try to shoot my goats Abigail?" he rumbled when she got closer.

"Of course not. My car backfired after I got startled when one of YOUR goats screamed at me as I drove up."

"Did you not notice 27 goats surrounding your car? They're not exactly hard to miss." The vein in his forehead was starting to pop out. Planting her hands on her hips she glared back.

"Of course I did!" She didn't. "But I didn't expect them to attack me when I got close."

There was no attacking. Did goats attack? They didn't strike her as aggressive creatures if they dropped to fake death at a loud noise. However, she wasn't about to admit that to this man.

"Goats don't attack. As you found out, they pass out when they're scared. They're called fainting goats for a reason." The sarcasm oozed out of him as his fists made their way to his hips, which wasn't good, as it drew her eye to his lower body.

There was no way this man was for real. The t-shirt pulled across his chest and bulged out the muscles there. It must be an optical illusion. Men weren't supposed to be built with that physique unless they went to the gym twice a day and Cole Pierson was not the gym type. Was this what working on a ranch did to a body? Because lordy, sign her up.

Cole cleared his throat and crossed his arms, making her eyes snap back to his face. One eyebrow rose above his ice-blue eyes.

"Are you done ogling me?"

Abby could feel the blood rush to her face, "I was doing no such thing! You have dirt on your shirt." Good Lord, bury her now.

"This is a ranch, Honey, there's dirt everywhere. Get used to it. And stay away from my goats." With that, he spun around and started to stalk away. Wait, that was it? No hello, here's the house, let me give you a tour?

"Wait!" She tried to race after him, but more goats got in the way. "Mr. Pierson. Cole. Wait!"

He spun back around, "what."

"What about the house?" He raised his eyebrow again at her. Did he think it was a form of communication? It wasn't.

"What about a tour? Where am I sleeping? Come to think of it, I'd like to see the rest of the ranch too. See how I can help out."

Sighing, he crossed his arms again, tucking his chin to his chest. As the silence stretched on, she wondered if he would answer her or turn and walk away. He lifted his head and glared at her. Man, this guy was broody.

"The house is there," he tipped his head towards it. "There is no tour. You sleep in any room that isn't the master. You don't need to see the rest of the ranch. You can't "help out" around here." The air quotes were a bit much, in her opinion, but she resisted the urge to roll her eyes.

"Okay, but I want to learn while I'm staying."

"I don't have time to teach you anything while you're here. You can stay in the house. Or you can go into town. Otherwise, stay away from the livestock-particularly my goats."

He turned to stomp off again, leaving her stunned. If he kept trying to escape this conversation, she was liable to sic one of these animals on him. Could they be trained to attack? Nothing serious, just a little nibble on his ankle?

"Wait, you can't be serious. You expect me to spend six months inside the house or in town, and never see any other part of the ranch? Even if I wouldn't go stir crazy, which I most certainly would, what could I possibly do to keep myself busy?"

"I don't give a damn Abigail. Learn how to knit for all I care."

"Knit. You want me to learn how to knit. Instead of teaching me anything to do with the ranch, that I'm 50% owner of," she deadpanned to him. Based on the glint that entered his eyes, being reminded she owned half of Sundown was a sore spot. Well, she wasn't thrilled at how this was going either.

"I don't care what the hell you do. You can't help on the ranch. You clearly don't know the first thing about how to work with animals. The only thing you'll be is a liability out there. No one has time to deal with someone who wants to brag to her friends she spent some time roughing it," Cole spit out.

"I don't want to freaking knit, and I don't want to brag about roughing it. I want to help. Is that too much to ask?"

This man was pushing all her buttons. Here she was, uprooting her life, leaving her job, moving, and he wanted her to stay home and darn his socks? He probably expected her to do his laundry and have dinner ready for him when he came home from a hard day of actual work.

"I don't care if you freaking knit! Just stay out of my way. There's no point in showing you how to do anything since you won't be here long enough to matter! It's obvious you don't know the first thing about being on a ranch. You thought you killed my goddamn goats! You don't even have the proper footwear to be out here! Stay in the house and when the six months are up, you can go back to your life like this never happened!" Cole turned around and strode away, muttering to himself as he went.

Arrogant, stuck-up, misogynistic, entitled ass!

Who the hell did he think he was? Sure, she hadn't been on a ranch, but it wasn't like she expected to run the damn place. She wanted this to be her fresh start like Muriel intended. She wasn't going to roll over and slink into the house, being seen and not heard.

Abby would do what she did best-research, learn as much as she could on her own, but first-proper footwear. She'd rectify that now then. With that thought ringing through her head, she headed back to her car, praying it would start. The goats roamed away, following Cole, so she didn't have to worry about running any of them over at least.

Luck was on her side and the car started the first time. She couldn't imagine having to ask him for a jump. She whipped it around and drove back towards town, intent on finding proper footwear for a ranch, whatever that meant. Abby would have to prove to him she was invested in this. That stubborn ass would find out how tenacious she was.

Chapter Five
Cole

KNIT? Who the hell told someone to learn how to knit?

Cole knew he sounded like an ass, but couldn't bring himself to feel guilty about it. She couldn't come in here and start demanding things, taking his precious time away from what needed to be done, like fixing the goat fence-again. He considered naming every one of them Houdini. They broke out of any pen he built. He'd reinforced the slats, built it taller, put chicken wire around the whole thing; everything short of locking them up in the barn, which wasn't a bad idea at this point.

Cole went into the barn to check on one of the horses who threw a shoe the week before, trying to avoid the other ranch hands. Thankfully, no one was around when their shouting match escalated, but there was still the possibility someone heard. He'd catch shit for sure if they had. He didn't raise his voice often, but there was something about that woman that pushed every single one of his buttons.

As he entered Lucy's stall, he couldn't help but grin a little. After hearing what he was sure was a car backfiring, but could have been a gunshot, he rushed to the house and saw her, and what a sight she was to behold. He hadn't noticed the goats, all on their backs or her ratty car covered in dirt. No, it was her, reaching out like she was going to pet one of them and bending over in that little yellow sun dress showing off shapely legs. He hadn't seen those at the lawyer's office, not that there was much he noticed about her, clouded by shock at the time. He froze in place at the view, instead of running over to demand she stop trying to manhandle his herd. The goat would have kicked her if she'd touched it.

Then he got angry. At her, at himself, at Muriel, and then he was yelling. It wasn't her fault the goats got out, but with this whole nonsense going on it was easier to take it out on her than to be rational. Based on how she acted the first time they'd met he'd thought she was quiet, the type to keep her head down and avoid confrontation. When she squared up and gave it right back to him, he was a little dumbstruck, and a little turned on, not that he would admit it.

The fire she'd spewed at him only worsened the situation, and made it hard to remember he shouldn't admire her. She was a good actress, that was all. At Harold's, she acted like an innocent little lamb. Here she was a raging lion. He had to remember she could turn it on and off at the snap of her fingers, or he'd get sucked into her game. That's all this was to her-a game.

But it was hard to forget the way her pupils dilated. When she planted those small fists on the curve of her hips it was all he could do to keep his gaze on her face. She couldn't have been much more than five and a half feet, but what she lacked in height she made up for in presence. No doubt she used her looks to her advantage, bamboozling all sorts of people out of their money, just like she had his poor aunt.

No use fawning over her. So she was beautiful. Plenty of gorgeous women running around. Not exactly in Sun Oak, at least none that weren't taken, but still. Wasn't like he was looking for anyone, especially someone like her. It didn't matter if her hair was silky, falling down her back in soft curls, or her eyes were chocolate brown that looked like he could drown in them, or her body...he shook his head, picked up a brush, and got to work.

Except for Muriel, there wasn't much use for a woman in Cole's life. A casual fling here or there was enough, but no one wanted to settle down in the middle of nowhere. At least not the women in Cole's life. They all left in the end, to chase something more exciting. Oh, they all thought it was an adventure in the beginning, but the novelty wore off before long. Sure didn't keep his Mama around.

Abigail would be no different. She'd leave this place with nothing but her memories if he had anything to say about it. No use looking for something that was never going to be there. Besides, she was a schemer. She was already trying to find a way to weasel her way on to the ranch, to 'learn'.

Cole scoffed, imagining her in her little sun dress trying to haul hay or feed the chickens. They would peck her ankles in those sandals, and then she'd come crying to him about it. He'd be lucky if she didn't sue him. Hell, he'd be lucky if she survived the next six months.

"Can you imagine her trying to ride you, Lucy? She'd flip right over the other side if she could even get up there in the first place. We'd have to bring out a stool for her."

Lucy nickered in response, swinging her head around to try to nip him. She didn't like being cooped up here.

"Well, aren't we ornery today? Try not to eat the new lady if she comes wandering back here huh? She'd want to send you to the glue factory."

His thoughts shifted as he checked Lucy's hooves. Even if arguing with Abigail was the most exhilarating thing to happen to him in years, he kept reminding himself she wasn't here for him, or for the ranch. She was here for the money, maybe more. They sure as hell weren't on the same side.

Abigail wanted something more than the payout waiting for her, he was sure of it. Why else would she want to tour the ranch? Either she thought this was a holiday or she was trying to get more money out of him. Maybe she thought she could score the whole thing. He didn't think she'd put her whole life on hold to check out the country life, she must be after something. Cole's gut told him she couldn't be trusted. She was a conniving little impostor who wormed her way here, and he'd be damned if he would let her get away it.

Chapter Six
Abby

"KNIT? Who tells someone that? Maybe I'll knit him a muzzle," Abby muttered as she swept through the aisles at the General Store in Sun Oak. The place was straight out of a western movie, offering a bit of everything, with footwear near the back. She almost didn't notice when she nearly plowed into a woman about her age.

"Sorry! I wasn't paying attention," Abby said. This day just kept getting better and better. Now she was taking out unsuspecting townsfolk.

"No problem," the woman replied, gripping her purse and smiling with deep red lips, "are you new to town? I haven't seen you around."

"Oh, this is the first time I've been to Sun Oak," Abby

said twisting around to face her.

The woman had at least four inches on Abby and could only be described as graceful. She was probably the type to glide, whereas Abby felt like she plodded everywhere, in heels, sneakers, flip-flops-it didn't matter.

"Passing through or. . ."

"No, I'm here for a couple of months."

Abby grew up in a small town, bigger than Sun Oak, but still a small town. She knew people would be curious about who she was and why she was here. She didn't know how comfortable she was with everyone knowing she was only here because of Muriel's will, but there wasn't any hope of keeping it quiet for long if it was anything like her hometown.

"Only a couple of months?" Her autumn green eyes twinkled playfully, making Abby think she already knew.

"Yup, just looking for a change of scenery." It was hard to make small talk with a stranger in the first place, but factoring in Abby was going for subtle as well, made it all the more difficult.

"Not a lot of places to stay around here."

"Ah, well, you know, small town." Abby glanced around, hoping no one was eavesdropping on them.

"I'm Gabriela Monroe, by the way." She tossed her long, dark hair over her shoulder and extended a hand. Yup, graceful.

"Abby. Abby Summers. It's a pleasure to meet you." Abby shook her hand, spying Gabriela's wedding ring wrapped around a finger.

"I confess, I knew who you were when you came barreling in here," Gabriela said with a mischievous grin.

Abby heaved a sigh. The situation was bizarre, especially with how Cole reacted to her, without having to worry about what others were saying about her.

"I figured as much. It's not easy to keep a secret in a place this tiny," she admitted.

"Nope. But don't worry. Most people are friendly. I moved here a couple of years ago. Started as a visit to my brother and I ended up staying after I met my now-husband, Zach. He owns Monroe's, the bar in town."

"I haven't been there. As a matter of fact, I haven't been anywhere other than Waterson & Avery and now here."

"And Sundown, right? Where you're staying?" Abby couldn't tell if Gabriela was being friendly or fishing for gossip.

"Mmhm."

"You must think I'm trying to get the gossip."

"Oh, no, of course not." Abby's cheeks reddened, trying to figure this woman out.

"Sorry. I promised I wouldn't ambush you and I'm failing

miserably." Gabriela's laugh bubbled out of her.

"It's okay. I'm sure everyone knows everyone here, so a stranger coming in will be the talk of the town," Abby relented.

"Well, you're not the only new person, fortunately. About two months ago we got a new doctor. He's young and cute so all the women are beating down his door, faking illnesses to see him. In all honesty, I'd think it was funny if I weren't the one scheduling their ridiculous exams to check their sun spots," she said ruefully.

"You won't have to worry about me. I'll have my hands full dealing with Cole," Abby said, forgetting her quest for subtlety.

"So, you encountered our local semi-recluse?"

"Recluse huh? You may be right about that. We didn't get off on the right foot-his goats were wandering about, then my car backfired, and they all fell over. I thought they were dead. It was embarrassing when they popped right back up as if nothing happened."

Now the shock had worn off, Abby could see how comical the situation was. She started to giggle, and Gabriela joined in, not holding back her amusement any longer.

"How did Cole react?" Gabriela asked when their laughter subsided.

"Oh terribly. He yelled at me. Told me I was a liability.

That I should learn how to knit. Knit! As if that's all a woman is good for."

"He yelled at you?" she hummed, looking thoughtful, tapping her painted fingernail against her lips.

"Yes! And he insulted my shoes. Allegedly, I don't have the 'proper footwear'." Abby rolled her eyes, waving a hand at her sandals, remembering the reason she stomped in here in the first place.

"I guess we'll have to get you some suitable boots then, won't we? Come on, I'll show you what kind to get." Gabriela linked her arm with Abby's and steered her towards the back.

Abby felt like she should object, but she needed help. She could use a friend too, if her interaction with Cole was any indication of how the next six months were going to go. She could use all the help she could get.

"So, what do you think of Sundown?" Gabriela asked, pulling a pair of boots off the shelf and handing them to Abby.

"I only saw the driveway, didn't even get inside the house before Cole was yelling at me and running roughshod over my wanting to learn about the farm." Abby took the boots and tried them on, scrunching her nose when they didn't fit right.

"Ranch, sweetie. It's a ranch, not a farm. Believe me, you

don't want to make that mistake."

"Of course. I knew that." She shook her head and picked up a pair with less heft.

"I'm a little frazzled over the whole encounter. I still can't believe he told me to learn to knit. Who does that? I mean, come on, this isn't 1890. Although, now I kind of want to learn, just to be petty. Make him a straitjacket." She snorted imagining Cole shackled in a knitted hot pink contraption.

"You could make him matching booties! It'd be adorable. I swear that man can get so stubborn about things. He never lets anything go." Gabriela snatched a pair of boots from Abby's hands. "Not those. They won't protect your ankles."

"How well do you know Cole? He doesn't seem the type to have a lot of friends, to be honest." Abby knew she was letting the few encounters with him cloud her judgment, but she couldn't help it. After all the hollering he'd done around her, she assumed he was a grump.

"My brother, Diego, is the foreman at Sundown, and my husband, Zach is his best friend," Gabriela gave her a side-eye, a smirk gracing her lips.

Mortified, Abby hung her head, concentrating on lacing up another pair of boots. Great, the first person she'd met in town, and she'd alienated her by bashing the only *other* person she'd met. This was going swimmingly. Had she made a mistake? Muriel spoke of this place like it held magical properties, but Abigail was her own personal ball of destruction, bred for interrupting peace and tranquility wherever she went.

"Of course he is. And here I've been going on about how much of an asshole he is, and he's your friend. I'm sorry. I'm sure he's a pleasant person…to other people. Just not me-for understandable reasons."

"Sweetie, please. I've known that man for five years now. I know what he's like. He tried to talk Zach out of dating me way back when. There's nothing you could say that would shock me about Cole Pierson. It's true, he's not one to yell, but it's a tense situation. With all the gossip floating around about Muriel's will, I'm surprised he didn't try to set you up in a tent on the western edge of the property," she laughed, tipping her head so her dark hair cascaded back.

"I wouldn't put it past him at this point," Abby muttered.

"Why do you think I wanted to meet you so badly? Anyone who could work Cole up so much before she arrived was sure to be someone I wanted to know. Besides, now you've got me. Between the two of us, I'm sure we can get Cole to pull his head out of his ass long enough to see you're not going to burn the ranch to the ground," she smiled at Abby expectantly.

"I don't know how I'll get him to not see me as a liability

but at least I'll have some kickass boots to stomp around in," she grinned, showing Gabriela the latest pair. They fit perfectly and covered all the parts that needed protection and it wouldn't be like slogging through a tar pit like the last pair.

"Perfect! Now, give Cole a couple of days to get used to the idea of you being around. He's all by himself in that big house. Might be perfect for him to have someone ruffle his feathers a little. In the meantime, talk to Diego. He's the one who runs most of the day-to-day stuff. He'll know where you can start learning things. He never turns away good help." She winked and started putting the boxes back on the shelves. "Now, let's pay for this and I'm treating you to lunch. We can get to know each other a little more."

Abby still didn't know if she'd made the right decision coming here, but the will to try with Cole wasn't there today. Gabriela obviously knew him better than she did, so taking her advice would be the wisest thing to do. Maybe this whole thing wouldn't be so bad if she gained a friend out of it. She'd wait to see if Cole would calm down and, in the meantime, she'd talk to Diego about how she could pitch in. If Cole still didn't want to let her in, she'd just have to convince him using a little kindness and a good home-cooked meal.

Chapter Seven
Cole

ALMOST a week passed before Cole saw Abigail again. At first, he thought he ran her right off the ranch, which would have been disastrous. He'd have to track her down and get her to return to fulfill the terms of the will. Later that first evening though he heard her car rumbling down the drive. He watched from his bedroom window as she disappeared with her bags through the front door. She stayed in her room the rest of the night. He was gone before she woke up every morning, and he never saw her when he came in for dinner. Maybe their spat changed her mind on helping out. It wouldn't be so hard to live with her if he never had to see her.

He woke up on Sunday to the smell of bacon. His alarm

was beeping incessantly, but all he could focus on was the aroma. It had been a long time since he had bacon in the morning before his chores. He didn't eat until he came in for a break and it was usually something quick. Muriel was the last person to cook him a proper breakfast. It was pointless to make a big spread for one person.

He got dressed and headed downstairs to see what trouble his new roommate had gotten into, bracing himself for the house being on fire. In the kitchen, was Abigail, swaying slightly, humming under her breath as the meat sizzled on the stove. Her small sleep shorts and tank top left a lot for him to peruse as he stopped at the bottom of the stairs.

He thought he'd convinced himself she wasn't that enticing, but it all went out of his head. Her chestnut hair was piled up on her head, pieces sticking out and falling out from her bun. She hardly looked put together, but the ease with which she moved about the room made it feel homey as if she belonged here. As soon as the thought formed, he shoved it out of his head. There was no way he could go down that road. Reminding himself she tricked Muriel into this and had no place here helped. He glanced away, trying to clear his head, but everywhere there were signs he wasn't the only one living here anymore.

An old Afghan blanket was thrown over one of the

couches. Her purse hung in the entry and those damn sandals rested by the front door. A laptop, books and paperwork were strewn across the dining table. She had well and truly taken over his space. How had she spread out so much in such little time, and without him noticing? She invaded his home and now she was cooking breakfast.

"What are you doing?" Cole asked as he stomped in. She jumped like she was startled, but she must have heard him come down.

"Good morning!" she chirped, glancing over her shoulder, "I'm making breakfast."

"I see that. Why?"

Turning back to the stove she said, "I figured you get up extremely early and you should eat something before you get to work, so I thought I'd make breakfast. Gabriela mentioned ranchers get up early and the books said it was a good way to start the day."

"Gabriela? How do you know Gabriela? And what books?" He couldn't believe it. She really was taking over every aspect of his life.

"Oh, we met when I went into town the first day. We've gotten together a few times this week for lunch. She's been so helpful," she beamed at him.

He went to the table and scanned the books: *How to Run a Successful Ranch, Cattle Farming: A Layman's Guide to*

Understanding Ranch Life and *Ranching for Dummies* were tabbed, notes scrawled on a legal pad. He didn't even know there was a *Ranching for Dummies* book.

"You can't be friends with Gabriela."

The last thing he needed was to hear from Zach how Gabriela thought this woman was the greatest thing to come to Sun Oak and Cole should give her a chance. He tore his gaze away from the mess to Abigail, who had a frown on her face. It didn't last though. She met his stare, smiled, and turned back to the stove, starting to plate up the food.

"Well, fortunately, you don't dictate who I can be friends with. Gabriela has been a lifesaver since I got here. I owe her a lot. Now eat up."

She slid the plate piled high with food in front of the stool at the kitchen island. It smelled delicious. The last thing he wanted to do was walk away, but no good would come from accepting food from a crook. She'd taken over his house. She was poaching his friends. He wouldn't accept food from her too.

Cole turned on his heel and marched towards the door. He couldn't help but glance back, only to see her face fall with tears in her eyes as she turned back toward the sink. Not wanting to be sucked further into the scheme she was cooking up alongside the bacon, he abruptly walked out the door.

* * *

* * *

He skipped his morning break, not wanting to see what new ploy Abigail came up with to reel him in. He kept seeing her face fall, tears welling in her coffee-colored eyes. He knew he hurt her feelings by not eating the food she obviously worked hard on. Guilt hit him every time he thought about her getting up extra early to start cooking. He didn't like making women cry, but this was the third time he'd seen her near tears. It didn't sit right with him, even if she was a manipulator.

Everyone noted how distracted he was most of the morning. Diego mentioned several times Cole's head was in the clouds. One of the newer hands asked if he got laid. The kid was mucking out the horse barn for that. After trying to latch a fence three times before it caught, he knew he had to do something. He needed to get away from the ranch and from Abigail.

Cole climbed in his truck next to the barn and drove past the house, determined not to check if her car was out front. He almost made it but glanced in his rear view at the last second to see it parked in her spot. At least he knew he wouldn't run into her while he was in town. He almost convinced himself that was the reason he looked at all by the time he turned out of the drive.

Pulling into the empty parking lot of Monroe's ten minutes later, Cole hoped Zach was there, even if the bar didn't open for another couple hours. He'd known Zach since they were babies. Growing up together, going to school, chasing girls. For as long as Cole could remember they had been best friends. There weren't many memories that didn't include Zach. Cole let himself in and took his usual stool, while he waited for Zach to wander in from the back. Not two minutes later Zach came around the corner, hauling boxes full of bottles of beer.

"Well, look who finally decided to show his face. Thought you'd be hiding out on the ranch some more with that pretty lady friend you got locked up there," Zach's blue eyes danced with delight. Ever since Cole told him about Abigail, Zach was having a field day, giving him shit about the whole thing.

"Screw you, man. This whole thing is 1000 times worse than I thought it would be," Cole griped as Zach handed him a beer.

"Easy there, you'll make me think you don't want to drink for free." Zach said, leaning against the bar. Cole flipped him off.

"First, she tried to kill my goats, and yelled at me, then she wanted to have an interactive experience with life on a ranch. Now she's taken over my house, leaving her stuff everywhere. She's got her hooks in *your* wife. And she tried to make me breakfast this morning."

Zach gasped, "oh no! Breakfast! The horror! Do you think she poisoned the eggs? A little arsenic as seasoning?"

"She probably did," Cole muttered. He didn't think she'd poison him, but with the way Zach was acting, he was blinded to the ramifications of having Abigail here.

"Man, she seems harmless. Gabriela has been talking about how helpful she's been. You know Gabby got a job at the doc's office? She's not the best with the computer system and Abby helped her go through it all. They came here one day for lunch too. She was nice. I think you're letting her involvement with Muriel's scheme cloud the way you're seeing her. Could it be she made you breakfast as a peace offering?"

"Of course, she was nice! Of course, she helped Gabby. Breakfast was a bribe, nothing more. She's trying to creep into every aspect of my life. I think she's trying to see if she'll be able to buy out my portion when the time comes." Cole didn't want to hear about how nice she was to everyone. She had some ulterior motive here no one else could see. A smile and a pretty face blinded them.

Zach scoffed, "Buy out your portion? I thought she was only in it for the money? You said she was poor and that was her motive for agreeing to this crazy stunt. Or is she in it for the vacation experience? You're going to have to settle on one thing to hate her for, instead of waffling. People might think you're fighting feelings for her."

"Crazy stunt is right. She manipulated Muriel into this, I know it. It's feasible she thought she could get Muriel to sign the whole ranch over to her, but Muriel still had enough sense to put some sort of roadblock in the way. I have to figure out how to keep her here for six months without her thinking she has any stake in my ranch. Get her to sell out her shares and then out of town. She's a city girl. She won't want to stay once she gets the cash."

Zach was shaking his head, but Cole hardly paid him any attention as he contemplated what Abigail's end goal could be. He was too busy coming up with a plan to be civil with her while still keeping in mind she could be trying to pull the wool over his eyes to entertain Zach's rational explanations for her actions.

"You dumbass. I can't believe you concocted this whole thing in your head."

"I may be a dumbass, but you'll see. She'll take you two down too when she screws me over. That woman is plotting something, and I'm going to figure it out. She's bound to slip up at some point."

"Do you have heat stroke? Did Trigger kick you in the

head? Is that why you're like this?"

Cole ignored him, saying, "I gotta get back before she burns the house down. Although, if I get her for arson that would help me get my ranch back."

"God help the woman who gets stuck with your stubborn ass. I hope you end up eating your words and begging that woman for a chance to be with her." Zach laughed again, throwing the bottles into the recycling.

"No chance of that happening in this lifetime. The last thing I need is another woman taking off for bigger and better things."

Cole waved to his friend as he walked out the door and to his truck. He'd bet all his shares in Sundown that woman was out to get something of his, but his heart wasn't one of them. He'd never let her near enough to fall for him.

Chapter Eight

Abby

ABBY tossed the eggs in the trash. No point in keeping them if Cole wasn't coming back. He wouldn't change his mind and come waltzing in, apologizing and asking for breakfast. He took after Muriel in that regard. It hurt when he walked away. She gave him space, like Gabriela suggested, but either he needed more time or he wasn't willing to give her a chance. Abby knew it was an unusual circumstance, but did he have to blame her for Muriel's decisions? She was as much a victim as he was.

She'd spent the last week picking Gabriela's brain and reading up on how a ranch operated. Reading and doing were two different things though. She'd hoped her peace offering would soften Cole up, and she could ask him again about learning some tasks around here. That was a dead end, so she'd have to take matters into her own hands.

She sat down to read through her notes from the past week. The books she'd picked up helped a lot, but she still didn't know what she'd actually be able to do. She didn't know how to ride a horse or help with calving, which she'd seen entirely too much of. While it was fascinating, she didn't know if she could handle watching a mama cow struggle to give birth. She started reading about stillbirth calves and ended up near tears.

Now though, she tried to focus on the things that seemed easy to pick up. She could feed the chickens. Mucking out stalls sounded terrible, but she was confident she could do it. Mending fences and herding cows though were way over her head. She hoped by the time October came around she'd at least get up on a horse.

After several hours of reading, Abby made her way upstairs to shower and change into a long sleeve shirt and jeans, even though it was hotter than the surface of the sun outside. She tucked her jeans inside her new boots she wore everywhere, hoping to break them in, so she wouldn't have blisters. Fixing her hair in the messy bun, she didn't bother with makeup. What was the point when it would sweat off her within ten minutes?

Outside, there was a decent breeze as she rounded the

house and set off for the big barn she'd seen her first day there. She noticed a pen ahead, all the goats safely tucked inside. They bleated as she passed. There was a large chicken coop, but most of the chickens were inside, taking shelter from the hot sun. The barn was painted a bright red, and two large doors were thrown open. There were stalls, mostly empty, along with a loft that held a massive amount of hay.

"Hello?" she called out, wanting to catch the foreman when Cole was gone. She'd seen him drive past the house as she was getting changed. That bought her some time before he came in huffing and puffing again, but if she had to go on a wild goose chase to find Diego, it would eat into her time for sure.

A man who looked like he spent hours under the sun came out of one of the stalls down the row. Immediately Abby could tell he was related to Gabriela, they had the same wide dark eyes that twinkled with mischief. The same sable-colored hair; noses mirror images of each other, complete with the same laughing eyes.

"Diego?" she asked and the man smiled.

"You must be Miss Abby! I wondered when I'd find you snooping around. Gabby said to keep an eye out. What can I do for you? You want a tour?" He was the complete opposite of Cole, his face open and friendly. How did two people so opposite work together?

"Hi! Gabriela told me so much about you. She said you might help me find something to do around here. A tour sounds like the perfect place to start."

"Well, let's go find you a horse and get going. I've got a couple hours before I have to check in on the cattle in the south field." He turned and started towards the back door of the barn.

"Oh, um, I don't know how to ride. I've never been on a horse, much less a ranch before. I was hoping we could walk?"

Diego tutted, "Don't think you'll want to walk Miss Abby. It's an awfully far way out to see some of this place."

"How big is this ranch?" she asked. She walked in the city when she missed the train for work. There was no way she was going to try to fake knowing how to ride, though she was dying for a tour.

"About 500 acres. It would take you about five hours to walk to the west field and then another five hours back. A little less if you're used to walking in this heat," he grinned. He seemed to smile a lot, based on the laugh lines bracketing his mouth. His dark eyes crinkled, deepening the surrounding grooves.

"Well, maybe a little tour around here? I was hoping I could learn to do some things rather than just sitting in the house learning how to knit." Her sarcasm blew right past

Diego.

"You don't strike me as the knitting type, but okay. I can show you around the barns for now. We could get you up on a horse, teach you a little about riding."

"Is there anything else I can do? Feed the chickens or learn how to mend a fence? Anything really. I've been reading up on it and I'd like to learn."

She smiled, praying he was in a generous mood. She didn't know what she'd do if he said no. She should have cooked Diego breakfast instead. He seemed more susceptible to a food bribery than Cole.

"Well, I always need more help. I'm sure there's something we can get you set up with. The chickens have been fed. Boss feeds them before the sun comes up. Takes care of feeding the goats too. I'll have a talk with him, see what you can do."

Shit. If Diego asked his boss, Cole was sure to shoot him down if only to spite her. If she could get something accomplished today, she could point to it, and maybe Cole would see she was serious, and ease up a little.

"Please, give me anything. I'm a fast learner, but I can't stay in that house anymore. I'm going insane." She didn't like begging, but desperate times and all that.

Diego laughed, "alright. Let's head over to the horse barn. We'll see what you can do. Horses always like a good rub down if nothing else."

He started off, Abby trailing behind him, and he pointed out things on the way to the horse barn. The pump house, another pen, which was actually called a paddock, for the horses.

He gestured towards a path that led into a grove of trees, "back there is the creek. Not real big, but good for swimming. The old homestead cottage is back that way too. Piersons bought this land, built the cottage, and started this ranch with little more than a dream and a couple head of cattle."

"Wow. I can't imagine having all that history in one place," she said.

"Lots of history around these parts. My grandparents came here from Mexico. Our parents taught us a lot about our culture, but it's blended with what they have here."

Diego walked to the doors and stepped inside where it was cooler. She could hear the horses shuffling about. Nerves shot through her body. They were bigger than she'd thought. A lot bigger, in fact. How she'd ever get up on one of them without a trampoline she didn't know.

"This is where we keep the horses. We mostly use them to herd cattle. Lots of places are using ATVs now, but Boss wanted to keep with tradition. They're docile, used to people-except for that one." He pointed to a stall at the end where a black horse poked his head out.

"That's Trigger, Cole's horse. Doesn't like anyone other than him, so I'd stay clear."

A deep brown head poked its face out of a stall next to her, making her jump.

"You sure you want to do this today? We can take it slow, don't have to get too close to them." Diego gazed intently at her.

Abby shook her head, "nope. I want to do this. Give me a brush or whatever and tell me how to not piss them off. I'll do the best I can and hope they don't kick me."

The horse shuffled closer, trying to nuzzle Abby's hair. She didn't move, not knowing what to do.

"Alright then. This is Lucy. She's ornery sometimes, but looks like she wants to meet you," Diego answered with another smile.

He grabbed two soft-bristled brushes, handing one to Abby. He opened the half-stall door, leading them inside. Lucy was beautiful, a deep chestnut brown with a mane of light browns running through the darker strands. Lucy swung her head around, snuffling at Abby's hand.

"Mierda, I think she likes you, Miss Abby." Diego shook his head and started brushing her, while Abby patted Lucy's head.

"What does 'mierda' mean?" she asked. She'd taken

Spanish in high school, which meant she knew how to ask where the library was and not much else.

"Means 'shit' Abigail." Abby whipped her head around. Cole was leaning on top of the stall door. "What do you think you're doing out here?"

Diego saved her saying, "Boss! I was showing Miss Abby the horses. She's a natural," he said, winking at her, "Lucy likes her."

Cole glared at Diego. She squared her shoulders and reminded herself she had every right to be here. Muriel made it clear in her letter Abby belonged. Just because Cole couldn't get on board didn't mean he could treat her, or anyone who talked to her, like shit.

"I told you I wanted to learn and Diego was kind enough to let me help."

Her voice shook more than she wanted, but at least she got it out. Where was her confidence from when she was defending herself about the goats? Her assertiveness when telling him he couldn't pick her friends? Oh, yeah, it went in the trash with the eggs.

"Come with me, Abigail." Cole turned and strode away, not waiting to see if she followed. She looked at Diego, who was busying himself with something on the wall. Knowing she'd get no more help there, she put the brush down and hurried after Cole.

"I'm not going to jump every time you call Cole." There, that was better.

"You're here now, aren't you?" he said as he continued to walk towards the bigger barn.

Snarky bastard. She couldn't tell what was going on in his head, his voice not giving anything away. Was he angry? Guilty? Did he want to apologize?

"Listen, I don't know why you want to help so badly, but we don't need it. You'll be in the way more than anything," he said, still not looking at her.

"Diego said you could always use the extra help. I'm not looking to milk a cow or rope some cattle, just feed the chickens, learn how to mend a fence. Something like that."

He shook his head, "we don't milk cows on this ranch. And we're not the kind that ropes cattle either, unless necessary. And mending a fence takes time, patience, and a certain amount of trust. If it's not done right, the cattle could get out and get hurt."

"Well, I can't mess up feeding chickens," she huffed, trying to keep up with his long stride. They were nearing the main barn. Abby knew the discussion would be over as soon as they were there.

"You wanna feed the goddamn chickens? Be my guest. I feed them at 5:30 every morning. Hell, I'll let you muck out the horse stalls. Not much you can screw up there, but it's not a pleasant job. A city girl like you won't like it much." He stopped inside the large door and glared at her.

She couldn't believe his ego. To judge he knew her when he hadn't asked anything about her. He hadn't done anything other than yell at her.

"I can get up early, and I don't give a damn how much shit it is, I can muck out the stalls. Just because I didn't grow up on a farm doesn't mean I'm a city girl ya know."

She knew she said something wrong as his face darkened.

"It's a ranch, not a farm Abigail. You would do well to remember that." With that he strode away into the twilight of the barn, leaving her there, cursing herself.

Chapter Nine
Cole

DIEGO wouldn't stop bugging him. It'd been three weeks since Abigail moved in and every time Cole crossed paths with his foreman he'd ask about Miss Abby. She left her mark on everyone she came into contact with. Zach was bugging him to give her a chance. Gabriela hadn't stopped dropping hints about this being 'something more', whatever that meant. Beverly, Adam's wife, at the feed store, asked when he was going to start bringing her on the supply runs. Townsfolk would stop him on his way to the bank under the guise of asking about the ranch, but talk always turned to her. Cole had talked to more people in the last couple weeks than in the last three years combined. He didn't want to socialize. He wanted to run his ranch and that was it. She was becoming a thorn in his side.

Every morning when he got downstairs, there she was, eating yogurt or making tea. She'd moved a hideous tea set on to his counter, all shaped like cows with tails as the handles. Every time he saw it, he shuddered. She would lace her boots up and cheerfully greet him on her way out the door.

He'd catch glimpses of her hair swinging from her ponytail, the rising sun glinting off copper tones as she fed the chickens. He'd see her greeting the goats as he rode past in his truck, and one day she'd been trying to herd them back into their pen. Cole should have stopped to help, but he couldn't bring himself to. He never saw her mucking out the stalls for the horses though. Shoveling shit must be too much for little miss city girl.

"Diego, who's been mucking out the stalls?" Cole asked as they herded the cattle to a new field one day.

"Ah, well Boss, I saw Miss Abby trying a couple weeks ago…" Diego paused.

"And?" he prompted.

"You can't actually expect her to clean up all that shit." Diego wouldn't meet his eyes.

"She was the one who wanted to help. Shoveling shit is the way she can help. Who's been doing it if she hasn't?"

"I've got Billy on it. And I've got Miss Abby feeding the

goats and putting fresh hay in the auxiliary barn for when the cows start calving. She's a natural, working hard."

It was bad enough everyone thought she was God's gift to their tiny ass town now that she bewitched them all. They all thought it was normal to let this interloper into their lives. Couldn't they see the damage she had done? She'd stolen half of his legacy, like a thief in the night. She knew precisely what to say and do to enamor them; blinding them to her true nature. If he didn't find some way to get her to show her devious ways soon, everyone would hate him. They'd blame him when she left. It'd be his fault their little ray of false sunshine ran back to the city. He couldn't help feeling he was fighting a losing battle.

He had to show her this wasn't a vacation. That ranch life was more than petting goats and feeding chickens. Fortunately, the perfect opportunity was right around the corner. Calving season was brutal for everyone. They separated the cows from the heifers in the auxiliary barn, so everyone knew which ones to keep a closer eye on. Once everyone left for the day though, Cole was on his own. He could have asked someone to stay on and help with checking during the night, but he didn't want them too tired the next day to do their other jobs. Abigail kept bugging him with all sorts of questions about it. She'd clearly been reading since she knew the basics. When he mentioned he thought reading was enough though she said, 'reading is not doing'.

"Do I get to help?" Abby asked one day, leaning against the counter next to the sink.

She was drinking her tea while cupping the udders under her cup. He had an irrational urge to smash the entire set. He was irritated from getting up every three hours during the night, plus running the ranch during the day. The stress, coupled with her incessant questions, grated on his already frayed nerves. The tea set might be the final straw.

"No," he growled.

"Can I watch?" Why did she have to constantly be in the kitchen when he was? She must be timing it to catch him on his morning break.

"Maybe."

He wanted her there if only to get her to see ranch life was messy and gross, not all fainting goats and pretty horses, but if he said yes too easily, she was sure to be suspicious. He'd been fighting her for weeks now. A complete 180 would make her wary. He had to ease into it, and afterward, he could get her to admit this was too much. Then she'd leave him be. Stop interrogating him. Stop 'helping'. Stop stealing into his life.

"Really?! I've been going through the barn to see them. I've read all about it. I tried to watch a video on it, but the internet kept going out, so I only got to see a blurry picture that looked like a messy Georgia O'Keefe painting."

"Not far off," he muttered, "fine, you can watch, but you have to stay out of the way. We don't want the cows to get more stressed than they already are and my guys have to be able to work without you distracting them."

Cole walked to the sink to rinse out his cup and his arm brushed hers. She shivered as if a sudden chill ran through her, but she didn't move. He set the cup down and backed away quickly. He had gotten a little too comfortable with her being here. Keeping his distance needed to be at the top of his list, otherwise, he'd get sucked into her path of destruction.

Abigail radiated excitement like the sun, pulling those close enough into her orbit. He couldn't be one of them, or he'd never get her to leave. He'd never *want* her to leave, and that wasn't a road he could go down. Eventually, she'd get tired of this life, the in and out of struggling to run a ranch this large day after day. She'd resent him for working so much like his mama had. She'd want more, like Jen had. That wasn't something he could give anyone.

Plus, she was only here for the money. She scammed Muriel out of half of the ranch.

The more he reminded himself of that, the more he wondered if Zach was right and this was only Muriel's scheme to break him out of whatever rut she thought he was in. He liked his rut. It was comfortable and normal.

He still didn't know much about Abigail-where she was from, what she did for a living, why she was here for real. Cole knew if he asked those questions though, got to know her, and she ended up being a con artist, it would gut him. So, he kept his distance, for both their sakes.

* * *

It was midnight, a week later. Cole hadn't let Abigail see much of the calving though. Most of the cows delivered quickly before she came through the barn. She kept asking him to tell her when it was happening, but he had enough on his mind without running around the spread to find her.

The last pregnant cow, a heifer, was taking her sweet time. He wasn't worried, as it was her first, but he kept an eye on her, sleeping in the barn most of the time to make sure she wasn't struggling. The heifer spent the last several hours in early labor, but when Cole saw the water bag, he knew it was time to wake Abigail. If she wanted to see everything, this was the perfect opportunity.

Cole knocked on her bedroom door and waited. He hadn't been in the room since she moved in but could imagine all her things strewn across every surface, just like the lower level. When she opened the door though, he didn't see the room at all he was so distracted by her. She was dressed in those damn pajamas again. Tiny, silky shorts showed off her legs and a barely-there tank top with no bra. He knew he was staring, but he couldn't stop. He should have expected it, but he was blindsided by those damn pajamas. Cole's eyes skimmed down and slowly up, taking in every inch of her. She cleared her throat and his eyes popped up to her face. She wore a little grin as she watched him, waiting for him to speak.

He looked off down the hall, avoiding her eyes, and said, "get dressed." He walked away briskly, adjusting himself as discreetly as he could. This woman was going to give him permanent blue balls. Five minutes later she tromped down the stairs, clothed in jeans and a long-sleeve shirt, and looked at him with anticipation.

"What's up Boss?"

Of course, she'd taken to calling him 'boss', complete with a little smirk on her full lips. He should say something, but that would only encourage her more. Every time she called him that though, a flutter would shoot through his chest.

"Hurry up. Last heifer is about to give birth." He led her out the door and to the auxiliary barn. The cow was pawing at the ground in the large stall, leaning against the wall now and then.

"What's her name?"

"She's a cow. She doesn't have one." Abigail apparently thought he named all his cows. And his goats, and his chickens and the random barn cat running around. He made his way into the stall, Abigail trailing close behind.

"Oh, but she has to have a name! What if you need to talk her through this? Are you going to call her 'cow'?" she said, a look of incredulity on her face. She crowded into the corner, far from the snorting animal.

"Fine, it's Betsy. This is her first calf, but she doesn't need to be 'talked through it'. They know what to do."

Cole sat down, back against the wall. Generally, he didn't have to do anything, but she was late, both with starting labor and the first stage. She'd been showing signs since earlier that evening and if she didn't get going, he might have to step in, but they weren't there yet.

"Aren't you going to do something?" Abigail asked, looking from him to the cow.

"Nope."

He leaned his head back and shut his eyes, hoping to get at least a little rest. A couple hours sleeping against a barn wall wasn't anything new for him.

"But what if she needs help? What if something goes wrong?"

Abigail was getting worked up. The last thing he needed

was two females huffing around, so he patted the hay next to him.

"Sit down. She's not going anywhere anytime soon. Either she'll do it on her own or I'll help, but right now she doesn't need you getting all worked up over nothing."

He didn't meet her gaze, he couldn't. He closed his eyes again, feeling her hesitation, but she sunk next to him. Her arm pressed against his, and he felt the heat sink into him slowly. She crossed her legs and her knee ended up resting against his thigh.

This was a bad idea. He should have left her freaking out in the corner. At least he could pretend she wasn't here then; that he wasn't so aware of how his body responded to her closeness. She sighed and thumped her head back against the wall by his shoulder, almost reaching his collarbone. Sometimes he forgot how small she was. If he pulled her into his lap, she could curl up like a cat, her head tucked under his chin.

Cole jolted himself upright. This wasn't just a bad idea; this was a horrible idea. He wanted her to see the messy parts of ranching, but if he couldn't get his thoughts under control, he'd end up doing something they'd both regret. Like kiss her. Great, now he was picturing what it would be like to kiss her. Would she pull away? Sink into him? Open up right away or make him work for it? At least if he was occupying her mouth, she wouldn't be asking questions. That'd be a sure way to shut her up.

Cole shot to his feet. Now he was the one freaking out. Watching a cow give birth was not sexy, yet all he could think about was Abigail and her body. The fantasies must be from sleep deprivation. She blinked up at him, and he prayed she didn't look down. There was no way she knew what he was thinking, thank god. She'd use it against him for sure. Or use it to tempt him more. He needed space.

He checked the time, noticing it was almost two hours since the heifer started, but she was restless now. She started bellowing and butting her head against the wall. He watched as she laid down on her side. Usually, that was a good sign but with all the other things she was doing, this wasn't going to plan.

"Shit." He looked at Abigail and tossed his phone to her. "Call Diego. If he doesn't answer, go down the line. Tell them to get here. Now."

He checked on Betsy. Dammit, now he was calling her by her name. Unfortunately, he had other things to worry about. Cole could hear Abigail trying to connect with someone, but no one was picking up. He knew a lot of them were sleeping, after the long week of births, but someone needed to answer now. He didn't want to have to intervene with only Abigail to help. She'd be useless.

"No one is picking up Cole. Do you want me to try again?" For some reason, she sounded calmer than she had when they first got in the stall. It was like the more worked up he got, the more settled she was. He took a deep breath, exhaling, deliberately trying to slow his heart rate.

"Try Diego again. If he doesn't answer, call the vet."

He patted Betsy's sides and tried to find out what was wrong. He could see the front hooves of the calf peeking out with each contraction, but there wasn't any progress. Her tail lashed back and forth and the bellowing continued. Cole heard Abigail talking to someone while he got gloves and other things ready. He didn't relish trying to reach in and yank the calf out with just the two of them, but if no one could get here, it was the only option. Hopefully, Betsy could push out the calf on her own with a little help.

"Um, so I got a hold of the vet. He said he was dealing with a thing with a horse. I mean, he was speaking gibberish, but he said he wouldn't be able to come for at least another hour. Which, I'm assuming, we don't have." Abigail bit her lip.

"Well Honey, seems like you got your wish. You wanted to help, now you're going to get your chance. I need you to go up by her head and try to keep her calm. Stay away from her hooves, she's not against kicking you."

Cole pulled the gloves up to his shoulders and lathered on

some gel. It wasn't the first time he needed to do this, but it never got any easier.

"What the hell are those for?" Her eyes were round, her pupils almost drowning out the chocolate brown in them.

"Gotta help get the calf out. Don't want to ruin my shirt now do I?" Cole chuckled; arms spread wide.

"You're going to stick your whole arm up her...okay. Sure, yup. Okay. Let's do this."

Abigail looked like she might puke. He prayed she had enough common sense to do it on the hay and not all over Betsy's head. The cow would lash out for sure, not to mention, he might puke too. She made her way around and settled by Betsy's head. He could hear her muttering something, and he strained to hear as he waited for another contraction.

"It's okay Betsy, you got this. Girl, this is nothing. This is the price you pay for letting some bull stick it in ya, but there's a light at the end of the tunnel sweetheart. Soon you'll have a cute little baby running around and pissing you off. It'll all be worth it in the end," Abigail babbled encouragement to the cow.

Cole couldn't help but grin. He'd seen a lot of cows in distress and this was the first time he'd seen someone trying to talk a cow through it. In most cases they would throw out a 'come on girl', but this woman was giving her a full-on pep talk. He didn't feel as lousy as he normally did in a situation like this. His anger towards Abigail was no match for her determination to get Betsy through this.

His grin faded though when he thought about what could happen after they got the calf out. Many times, they didn't make it-either being stillborn or from complications after. He was sure Abigail would lose it if this calf was stillborn. It wasn't ideal, he hated when it happened, but it was how things worked sometimes. He wanted her to see this was hard, but he didn't want her to experience that. She'd blame herself too, thinking if someone else was here it would have lived. That's not how it worked, but she wouldn't believe him. He hadn't given her much reason to.

Determined to move this along, he reached in when a contraction hit. He pulled the front legs, hoping he could move the calf down a little. A nose poked out and went right back in. Two more times he pulled with the contractions, all while Abigail got a little louder, yelling over Betsy's hollering. At last, the whole head emerged with the front legs, and he let go. If Betsy could do the rest from here, it'd be better for both the heifer and her baby. Minutes passed and the cow slipped free straight on to Cole's lap, covering him in blood and fluid. It looked up at him and bleated a little.

Suddenly, Abigail laughed. A full-body hoot, tipping her head back and hugging Betsy's head, which made its way into her own lap. Tears were streaming down her face, and yet he was caught by her beauty at that moment. The anxiety slipped away as he chuckled, grabbing a blanket to cover the cow. Betsy mooed, trying to turn and see her baby, so Cole picked the calf up and brought her around. Mama needed to clean it off if she could, but he knew she was tired. Immediately though, Betsy started licking the calf's head.

"Is it a boy or a girl?" Abigail asked, still chuckling and wiping her eyes with her sleeves.

"It's a girl." His lips pulled up, staring down at the three of them, feeling something move in his chest. Like a missing piece slotting into place.

"Oh! What should we name her?" Abigail was petting Betsy's head as she continued to bond with her baby.

Oh no.

Chapter Ten
Abby

"WHAT should we name her?" Abby asked again, glancing towards Cole and back to the cow, a grin still splitting her face. Even with the fear and stress of the whole night, she felt more alive than ever. She never knew watching a calf being born would be so exhilarating, like being part of something bigger.

Abby had done it. She finally felt like she belonged somewhere, just like Muriel said. There was something magical about this place, something that fed her soul. It was gross though. There was blood and fluid everywhere. Her eyes traveled the length of Cole up to his face. His entire front was wet from the calf. So much for the gloves helping save his shirt. But when she got to his face, he was wide-eyed and anxious.

"What's wrong?"

She swung her gaze back to Betsy and the calf. They seemed fine. Betsy rolled a little to reach more of the baby to clean it off. They looked like any other nature show birth she'd seen over the years. Not that she knew what could be wrong, but they seemed healthy in fact. Was something else supposed to happen? Had she made a mistake?

"You can't name the calf," he said, still looking at her with trepidation.

"What? Why not? You named Betsy. Don't you think her baby needs a name too?"

This man was so confusing, never seeming to be able to make up his mind. He ran hot and cold so much he was giving her whiplash with his mood swings. Sometimes she felt she was making progress with him, and he'd turn back into Mr. Asshole Extraordinaire and give her the cold shoulder for the rest of the week. She couldn't figure out what his problem was with her, other than blaming Muriel's decisions on Abby. She knew Muriel's will threw a wrench in his plans, and it wasn't easy to let someone he didn't know be in his house, but he needed to get over it. Abby was as much a victim to Muriel's scheming as he was. He couldn't keep blaming her for something that wasn't her fault.

"You can't name it." He glanced off across the barn,

avoiding her eyes while she climbed to her feet.

"Why not? I was part of this, I want to name her."

There was something he wasn't telling her. Why would he care if she named the calf? She wasn't asking him to be the daddy. That thought derailed her though, imagining Cole with a small child, teaching them to ride a horse, showing them the new calves, and pranking the goats to faint and go legs up. She shook her head. That wasn't a dream she would ever be part of. This man didn't want her near his ranch, much less mothering his babies. Abby's eyes shot wide.

Mothering his babies?!

What the hell was she thinking. She didn't want to date the man, much less marry him. Great, now she was thinking of marrying him. This was not where this whole deal was going. She needed to stop thinking about him like that and remember he hated her, or at the very least wanted her far away from him. Cole wasn't the type to nurture and care for anyone, much less her.

Bet he could take care of something for you though.

No, don't think about him like that.

She imagined him stripping out of his shirt and shimming out of his worn jeans. Stalking towards her while his eyes darkened with lust. She could feel her cheeks starting to heat. The last thing she needed was for him to figure out where her mind wandered off to.

"I want to name her," she said again, trying to erase the image in her mind. He was covered in goo, gloves still encasing his hands. This was the least sexy she'd ever seen him. She would not think about how he still looked like the perfect specimen; she erased those thoughts from her mind.

Cole went to run his hand through his hair but stopped looking at the gloves covered in blood. He peeled them off and tossed them over the stall door before he looked back.

"If you name it, you'll get attached. And if you get attached you won't take it well when I sell her." Cole had the decency to look troubled by the thought at least.

"Sell her? You can't sell her! She was just born! You can't tear a baby away from its mother like that!"

"Good god woman, I don't mean right this instant! She'll get sold after she weans. I'm not that much of an asshole." This time he did run his hand through his hair. Abby winced, hoping he wasn't spreading goo on his head.

"Well, I'm glad you can agree you're an asshole most of the time, but you can't just sell her. Look at her!" Abby gestured to the pair at her feet. The calf was mostly clean and starting to tuck its legs underneath it. "We went through a traumatic experience here! You can't get rid of her like none of it happened!"

Cole rolled his eyes but still wouldn't look at her or the pair on the floor. The silence stretched between them while the calf bleated and Betsy mooed. Suddenly, the calf pushed itself up, wobbling from the effort to stay upright. Abby's eyes filled with tears again. She didn't care what Cole said. This was her moment. If she needed to buy the calf herself, she would.

"Annabelle," she stated reverently. Watching the baby try to take a step and wobbled again.

"What was that?" Cole's eyes were fixed on her now.

"Her name is Annabelle, and she's going to grow up and be amazing," she said with awe.

Cole hung his head, pinching the bridge of his nose. Again, she hoped the glove didn't have a hole in it. He'd go blind getting goop in his eyes for sure.

"Dammit Abigail," he groaned, hanging his head before he turned toward the stall door.

"Where are you going?"

"I'm going to get cleaned up. Then I'm going to bed, but don't think I'm not selling that calf when the time comes," he huffed, leaving her to watch Betsy bond with Annabelle.

* * *

The days after passed bit by bit. Abby checked on Betsy and Annabelle every day until they were moved to pasture. With the rough beginning, Abby worried about the pair, but

Annabelle seemed to be thriving, and Betsy was back to her normal self. Diego put them in a nearby field so Abby could walk to them whenever she wanted. The ranch hands stopped by to give her updates on the pair. Everyone but Cole. He was back to avoiding her. When he was forced to see her, he was short, to the point, and wouldn't look at her.

Her stomach turned more than it should whenever her thoughts drifted to him, which was a lot more than she'd like. She thought she broke through some of his barriers, proved she was capable of helping, but him pulling away again hurt. She tried not to think about why she cared so much.

Abby met up with Gabriela and Zach for lunch at Monroe's one day. She tried to keep Cole out of the conversation, but with how they were all intertwined it didn't last. She confessed to them how hard it was, not knowing where she stood with him, but Zach was quiet. Abby didn't like putting them in the middle. Zach was his best friend, after all. So, she changed the subject. Telling them she'd figure things out, and if she couldn't, well, she only had a little over four months left. Cole wouldn't have to see her again after that. For some reason that thought made her chest twinge.

A new day dawned and Abby was at the chicken coop. It was early, the sun skimming the horizon when Diego's truck came bumping up the road towards her. She didn't know where Cole went off to. She didn't think he was sleeping at the house most nights. If he was, he was coming home long after she retreated to her room and gone long before she got up, which was extreme, since she was getting up at the ass crack of dawn. It was more likely he found another place to hide.

She waved to Diego and the kid in the passenger seat next to him. They both waved back and parked.

"Hola Miss Abby!" Diego jumped out of the cab with a grin. The teenager, who couldn't be more than fourteen followed him, apprehension clear on his face.

"Hey, Diego! You're here early. I'm about done with the chickens. Then I'm off to try to round up the goats again. I think they got into the auxiliary barn last night. Little buggers never stay where you want them to," she said with a laugh while she spread the feed at her feet.

"They're little shits. If they weren't so good at grazing the fallow fields, I'd tell Boss to get rid of them. This is Brayden. Come over here mijo. Say hello to Miss Abby." Diego grabbed Brayden's arm and tugged him to the fence.

"Good to meet you Brayden! Are you working here now?"

Abby could see how nervous he was. His sandy blonde hair fell into his brown eyes, which she only saw a flash of before he looked at his feet. His slim build would bulk up while he was here; he looked like a stiff wind would blow him into the next county at the moment.

"Yes ma'am. Off school for the summer and Mr. Pierson said I could start learning the ropes around here. I've been trying to get him to take me on for two years. He said I needed to grow a little more though." She saw a flash of a grin before he ducked his head again.

"Miss Abby, I thought you could show him what you've been doing. Get him started on something small before we throw him to the wolves with the other ranch hands. They'll eat him alive at this point." Diego chortled to himself. She wondered if he was ever in a bad mood.

"Of course. I'd love to show him around. Brayden, why don't you come in here and you can help me finish with these chickens. I'll give you a tour when we make our way over to the aux barn."

Brayden went over to the door, chickens attacking his shoes as soon as he stepped in. Diego waved as he hopped back in his truck and drove away.

"Well, this won't do Brayden," she said, looking down at his shoes. "You need to get some proper footwear if you're going to be working on the ranch. Tennis shoes aren't going to protect your feet. You'll need steel-toed boots. We'll go down to the General Store after we're through with the goats and get you some."

She didn't like how much she sounded like Cole, but he had been right. Shoes had no place on a ranch. She needed to get Brayden some boots before Cole came around. As soon as the thought crossed her mind, his truck came from the path that cut through the trees.

Dammit. Maybe the chickens will be enough to cover Brayden's feet.

Cole pulled his truck right up beside the coop and leaned out his window.

"Brayden," he barked, "what the hell do you have on your feet? And why are you bugging Abigail?"

Brayden's face fell, and he tucked his chin to his chest. Did this man have no people skills whatsoever? He was fine with the others working under him. No one in town seemed to have a problem with him. It was clear he had a problem with her though, or anyone who associated with her. She could tell Brayden was nervous enough starting, he didn't need Cole breathing down his neck because of her.

"Morning Boss. I'm going to show Brayden around, we're going to get the goats back into their pen, and next we're going to get him some boots. He didn't know what kind to get, so he asked for help instead."

Her little white lie wouldn't hurt anyone. She didn't want to drag Diego into this either. Cole's remarks made it obvious he didn't like that Diego was so friendly with her. No need to make it worse between them. Cole stared at her. She didn't know what he was waiting for. After a minute he sighed and looked back to Brayden.

"Get boots and find Diego. You need someone who knows what they're doing to show you around."

Subtle. She saluted him smartly as he narrowed his cobalt eyes at her before he drove away without a backward glance.

Brayden turned to her, wide-eyed, "is he always like that? He was super nice every other time I talked to him in town."

"Well, he's got to be the boss out here. Can't have everyone questioning you when you're running things."

Abby went back to spreading feed. There might be issues between Cole and her, but she wasn't going to undermine him to his employees. It was one thing to bitch to Gabriela or Zach, but to the people he worked with would be spiteful, but she was still sticking to her plan for Brayden.

Showing Brayden around was a lot more fun than she thought. She could tell how eager he was to learn everything. He prattled on about school, his parents, his younger sister, his friends, girls-everything under the sun. He blushed easily and ducked his head whenever he was nervous.

Brayden reminded Abby a lot of herself at his age. Fascinated by everything but terrified of screwing up. She knew she worried more than she should about what people thought of her, and she was in her twenties. Cole's attitude towards her didn't help either. She knew she shouldn't care, but she wanted his approval. She wanted him to see her as confident and capable and like she belonged.

They got the goats back in their pen and went to the house to get her car. It was covered in dirt and still tended to backfire, but what mattered was it ran. Gabriela kept telling her to buy a truck, but what would she do with it when she left? There was no need for a truck if she couldn't stay on the ranch. She kept pushing the thought of leaving off, trying to focus on the here and now.

"This is what you drive Miss Abby?" Brayden eyed her car apprehensively.

He'd picked up Diego's nickname for her as quickly as the others. She tried to tell them to call her Abby, but they all ignored her. At least they weren't calling her Abigail, like Cole. She swore he did it to bug her, but she was getting used to it. Realistically, it would be weird if he started calling her Abby now.

"She's reliable…most of the time. Gets me from point A to point B and that's all I need. No reason to get rid of something that isn't broken." Abby climbed into the driver's seat and cranked the engine, but nothing happened.

"You sure it runs?" Brayden eyed the car, hanging on to the open passenger door.

"Most of the time it starts right up. Give her a bit." She

turned the key again, but it wouldn't even turn over.

Of course, Cole's truck came around the house right at that moment. She couldn't catch a break. He'd been making snide comments about her car since she moved in. Pulling up next to her, he rolled down his window, waiting for her to acknowledge him.

"Get in," was all he said.

She wanted to argue, but Brayden was making his way to the pickup. Sighing she rolled up her window and got out to climb into Cole's truck. This should be fantastic.

Chapter Eleven

Cole

COLE navigated his truck down the dirt roads, trying to avoid the potholes. Every time they hit one, Abigail shifted into him, sending electric shocks down his arm and thigh. He had not thought this through when he told them to get in. Of course, his truck had to have a bench seat, and of course, Brayden would put her in the middle. She was the smallest, and fit the best wedged in between them, but it didn't stop him from glaring at Brayden every time she slid back towards the middle. He pulled up to the feed store and turned off the truck.

"I got some supplies to pick up. You two head over to the General Store and get some proper boots. I'll meet you back here when you're done." Cole didn't look at either of them as he climbed out and walked inside. He went up to the counter towards the back of the store, seeing Adam, the owner, working.

"Hey there Adam. I'm here to pick up Sundown's order for this week." There was a tingling on the back of Cole's neck, and he glanced behind him. Abigail and Brayden followed him in and were standing there, waiting. He turned to them and crossed his arms over his chest.

"I thought you two were going to the General Store." He watched as Abigail bit her lip. He wished she'd stop doing that. It put thoughts in his head he desperately needed to avoid.

"We're going to help you load up, and we can all go over together. I don't want to pick out the wrong boots for Brayden." She bit her lip again and peeked behind him at Adam, who was watching the whole scene. No doubt the entire town would know they came to the feed store together by the end of the day. Adam's wife was more than a bit of a gossip. She'd been trying to corner Cole every time he was in town to get the scoop on Abigail.

Cole noticed she went from asking him for things to telling him what she was going to do. Her confidence was growing around him, and he was more than a little annoyed with it. If she started thinking she could tell him what to do, because she owned half the ranch, he'd have more problems with her than he already had. It was hard enough to keep her off his mind as it was.

"I'm sure Brayden can handle it. He knows what he needs to get, don't ya kid?" Cole frowned at Brayden, trying to send the message he should get Abigail out of here. Cole didn't want to be sniping at each other in front of the kid.

"Uh," Brayden stammered, swinging his gaze between the two of them. "I'm not sure Mr. Cole." Brayden's eyes settled on Abigail, and he tucked his chin to his chest, and his cheeks flushed. Dammit, she got to him too.

"It's Cole, not Mr. Cole. Go get boots. Now." He turned back to Adam, hoping the pair would take the hint. Of course, Abigail couldn't just do what he wanted. She pushed and pushed until she got her way. They called him stubborn, but she took the cake.

"You should think about being a little nicer to him. He's only fourteen and trying the best he can. Are you going to turn down our help because you don't want me here?" At least she had the decency to lower her voice, but Cole was sure the owner could hear everything she was hissing at him.

Cole sucked in a deep breath and closed his eyes. He hoped if he ignored her, she'd go away. Cole had shit luck because she pushed past him towards the counter and stuck her hand out to Adam.

"Hello! I'm Abby. I'm staying at Sundown. You have an

order for us?" She shot a wide smile at Adam, acting like Cole wasn't even there. He tried to temper his reaction, to hide how livid he was. How dare she come in and take over. Every day she took a little more of his life. He thought staying at the cottage would put some distance between them after the whole Annabelle incident, but it was like no time passed when they were thrown together again. She burrowed her way into his brain and wouldn't leave.

"Welcome to Sun Oak, Abby. I'm Adam, owner and all that. We do have an order. I'll have my son Jake get it ready and bring it out to the truck. Same order next week Cole?" Adam shot a wink at Abigail before turning to Cole, suppressing a smile. Oh, the town would hear about this for sure.

Cole nodded, not trusting himself to speak, and spun around, back to the front and out the door. He was halfway down the block heading to the General Store before Brayden and Abigail caught up with him. They were chatting back and forth as if they were the best of friends, which only put Cole in a worse mood. They marched inside and to the back of the store, but Cole couldn't suppress the groan when he saw Gabriela talking to Mary, the owner, at the registers. This is why he wanted them to split up. A small town like this, they were sure to run into everyone Cole would rather avoid.

"Abby! Sweetie, I was going to call you! What are you

doing in town?" Gabriela's dark eyes slid to Cole, a smirk playing on her lips. He rolled his eyes and tried to ignore the suggestive look she was giving him. For some reason, Gabriela had in her head Abigail was perfect for him. She kept making comments about how cute their kids would be. He suppressed a snort. As if he'd ever have kids, much less with Abigail. She hated him, and with good reason.

Cole grabbed Brayden's elbow and led him to the boots, leaving Abigail and Gabriela to catch up. If she was occupied, perhaps they could get out of here without another argument. He grabbed the same boots he was wearing off the shelf and shoved them into Brayden's arms. As the kid started to sit down to try them on, Cole yanked him back up and pushed him towards the front.

"No need to try them on. They'll work." Brayden blushed and stumbled more than normal, but they needed to get out of here. Cole led him back to the registers where the women were still talking, but as soon as they stepped up, Abigail broke off her sentence and looked at them. Cole wished Mary would ring them up already, but she was staring at them open-mouthed.

"Brayden, dear, are those the right size?" Abigail put her hand on his arm. He looked a little like a fish out of water. Cole didn't think he was a scary guy, but manhandling the kid probably didn't help.

"Uh, I'm not sure, Miss Abby, but it'll be fine," he stuttered out, glancing at Cole before looking at his feet and blushing again. Cole closed his eyes briefly and then grabbed the box off the counter, pulling Brayden back towards the aisle.

"What size kid?" Cole crossed his arms over his chest and looked at Brayden's feet as if they would come to life and tell him.

"Size 10, sir." Brayden plopped on the bench.

Cole grabbed the right size and started towards the front again, Brayden scrambling after him. Once again, Abigail and her new best friend were talking as Cole put the box on the counter. Mary started to ring him up when Cole overheard what the women were talking about.

"Friday sounds great," Abigail said, "I don't know if my car will start though. It wasn't earlier." As he peeked out of the corner of his eye, he saw her bite her lip again. She needed to quit that.

"Oh, I can pick you up. We'll get Zach to give you a ride after he closes up. Then we can drink without worrying about driving back," Gabriela answered beaming.

Great, now they were making plans to go to Monroe's. At least they couldn't get into too much trouble with Zach looking on. He'd be able to spend some time alone in his own house tonight at least. The cottage wasn't bad, but the water never got above lukewarm. A hot shower sounded perfect after dealing with this fiasco all day.

The women hugged as Mary bagged up the shoes. Turning around, he walked out of the store, once again leaving Abigail and Brayden to catch up. Cole needed to get back to the ranch before he did something stupid, like grabbing Abigail and pinning her against the post office and pulling that lip she kept biting between his teeth. By the time he got back to his truck, Jake was finished loading the supplies, which made Cole wince. Typically, he helped Jake load, but he was so intent on getting out of town he completely forgot.

"Thanks, Jake. Appreciate it," Cole said, clapping the teenager on the back. Jake was a good kid, graduated from high school in May, and planned to stay around Sun Oak to help his dad.

"No problem Mr. Pierson! See you next week." Jake waved and took the empty pallet back into the store. Cole told him over and over to stop calling him Mr. Pierson, but Jake would smile, nod, and continue to call him it. Cole leaned against the driver's door, waiting for the others. He could see them stopped in front of the post office, talking to Brayden's mom. They owned the diner one street over and had the best rhubarb pie, but it had been a while since Cole had been by. Abigail hands flailed wildly, her ponytail flipping back and forth as she talked. She was smiling, so she couldn't be talking about him. Brayden blushed and looked at his feet, but smiled. The last thing he needed was the kid to develop a crush on Abigail. He didn't need a green kid distracted by a pretty face.

Like her pretty face distracts you?

I'm not distracted by her face. Or her body.

Sure, which is why you're now thinking about her body, like how those jeans cup her ass.

Great, not only was he arguing with the voice in his head, but he was also thinking about her ass. He needed to get out of here before someone noticed his pants didn't fit so well anymore.

They waved goodbye to Brayden's mom as Cole hopped in and started the engine before they were even close to the truck. Abigail slid over the bench towards him, and he tried to subtly squish himself against the door. She gave him a confused look as she buckled her seat belt, but he stared out the window before backing out and making his way home.

* * *

The shower was bliss, even if it was cluttered with Abigail's shower things everywhere. Who knew women needed so much stuff to get clean? She had at least three bottles in here, and they all smelled like gardenias, whatever those were. Plus, her pink razor sat on the shelf under his body wash. He had half a mind to throw her shit into the sink. Then he'd stop imagining her in here, getting naked and soapy. He shook his head and rushed to rinse and towel off.

Abigail left an hour ago to meet up with Gabriela for some type of girl's night. He had the house to himself. The problem was, he had no idea what to do. If it was a normal night, he'd fix himself dinner, do some paperwork, and head to bed, but after staying at the cottage for so long, he was restless.

Cole tried to find something to eat, but he couldn't bother with cooking. He turned on the TV, but there wasn't anything on. He tried picking up a book, but his mind kept wandering to Abigail and what she was doing. Was she drinking? Did they eat beforehand? Was she playing darts? Please god, let her not be playing pool. He'd seen her getting in Gabriela's car earlier, and she'd been wearing a blue sun dress. It wasn't particularly short, but if she was bending over a pool table…

He threw the book on the coffee table and leaned his head back on the sofa. He shouldn't be thinking about Abigail, or who was looking at her. It wasn't like they were dating. She could flirt with whomever she damn well pleased. Didn't make any difference to him. Then why was he suddenly furious at every guy in the bar who was sure to be checking her out.

What if she brings someone back here? Shit.

There was no way he was going to sit and watch her bring some douchebag here. He had to go to the bar. He was hungry, and he could keep an eye on Abigail and make sure she didn't take a stranger home. They'd likely steal something on their way out. That was the only reason he was going. Mind made up, he went to change and head out to Monroe's.

Chapter Twelve

Abby

ABBY hadn't been on a girl's night out since college. Five years was a long time to go without friends her own age. She'd forgotten how nice it was, but in the silences, she still missed Muriel. The older woman had been exactly what she needed after her parents died. Most of her college friends hadn't known how to be around her anymore. She went from carefree to someone who had responsibilities of a much older adult in the blink of an eye. They tried, but they didn't understand what she had gone through. Muriel did.

She traded in her bar-hopping for cups of tea on a porch and her late nights out for early morning commutes. She moved away from her college town and sold her childhood home to buy a house in the city two states away. A fresh start was exactly what she needed at the time, and for a while it was okay. Abby survived, but Muriel was right, she hadn't been living. Sitting across the table from Gabriela, laughing at the pranks she pulled on Diego, was a breath of fresh air. She missed this.

"So, Abby, my friend. Tell me. What is going on with you and Cole?" Abby had tried to steer the conversation away from talk of Cole, but Gabriela was persistent.

"Not a damn thing. I haven't seen him in days. He hasn't been staying at the house, and I almost never see him around the ranch. I'm sure you see him more than I do. He's here every night instead of coming home, right?" She hadn't planned on saying anything but the annoyance bubbled out of her.

"Oh sweetie, he hasn't been coming here. I haven't seen him at Monroe's in a while. He's come over for dinner a couple times, but he's been absent around town lately too." She scrunched her nose, looking concerned.

"Oh. Okay. I'm guessing he's out. You know, other places. Away from town." Abby stared at her drink. Where was he sleeping if he wasn't at the house, and he wasn't with his friends? Was he at a woman's house? Picking up random women at a bar and going home with them instead? Was she that terrible to be around he felt he needed to stay away? She could look for another place to stay in town, instead of staying at the ranch if it was a big deal. She'd have to ask the lawyer if that was possible though.

It hadn't even crossed her mind she might be cramping his sex life by moving in. He was gorgeous in a rugged way. He couldn't possibly have any trouble finding a woman to warm his bed. Those thoughts made her stomach twist, although she tried to convince herself it had nothing to do with her feelings for him and everything to do with guilt over intruding upon his house.

"I'm sure it's nothing, Abby. Maybe he's staying at the cottage. You know, getting some alone time. He hasn't had anyone in his space since Muriel left. He hasn't dated much since Jen. I wouldn't think he was out trolling for tail to get away from you." Gabriela didn't look entirely convinced, but it was nice she tried.

"Wait, who's Jen?" She hadn't met anyone named Jen in town and no one brought her up before now.

"Jen was Cole's high school sweetheart. I don't know the whole story, but she wanted to go to college and when Cole told her he needed to stay here she left. She hasn't been back since, as far as I know. I wasn't here then, but it was a big enough thing Zach told me not to mention her to Cole ever." She glanced at her husband who waved. They waved back and Abby tried to push the whole thing from her mind. It wasn't any of her business what happened to Cole over a decade ago.

"So, you know how I took the job with the new doctor?" Gabriela asked, changing the subject.

"Yeah, how's that going?" Abby helped Gabriela with the computer system, but he hadn't been around.

"Oh fine. Doctor Dan. He's cute. Like super cute. And very kind. One of those boy-next-door types." She took a drink from her straw while Abby raised her eyebrow. She was madly in love with Zach so there had to be a reason for this. "And he's single."

There it was.

"Single huh? Well, good for him." Abby stirred her drink and looked around the bar, trying to avoid her friend's gaze. The last thing she wanted to do was go on a blind date with her best friend's new boss, despite the fact he was a doctor.

"When was the last time you were on a date, Abby. A real date." Gabriela's gaze pinned her in place, demanding her to try to lie.

"Uh, well, it's been a while, almost six months."

"And how was it?"

"It was okay." Gabriela raised her eyebrow. "Okay, fine. It was terrible. He was a data entry supervisor, living over his parents' garage. He talked about his DnD group nonstop and smelled like corn chips. Oh, and he asked if I wanted to go back to his "apartment" and meet his five ferrets because he couldn't go out with me again if they didn't approve." She buried her head in her hands, mortified.

Gabriela looked aghast, "I'm a little afraid to ask, but before that?"

"There was the frat boy who wore so much cologne I thought I was in a body spray ad, the douchebag who told me if he paid for my meal, he expected a blow job at the end, the guy who wore a wife-beater and, *of course*, forgot his wallet. Oh, and the coup de grâce, the one who showed up in a full suit of armor." Dating apps had not been kind to her.

"Dios Mio."

It was one thing to hear all the crazy internet dates she'd been on, but it was a lot more to be there, sitting across from someone who kept jingling every time he reached for his water glass.

"All the more reason to go out with someone normal. With a normal job, that will not proposition you at the end of the night." Gabriela sucked more of her drink down and waited. Abby shuddered, reliving some of the more vivid dates she'd been on, watching the other patrons laugh at their tables while 80s hair band music played in the background.

The door opened and in strode Cole, because of course. Dammit, why the hell did he always have to look so good? Couldn't he wear a potato sack? It should be illegal to walk around in those jeans and that white t-shirt. He wasn't trying to look sexy, but it oozed out of him.

He marched right for the bar, not bothering to look around. Did he know she was here? No, of course not. If he knew, he wouldn't have come. A coincidence of fate. Thinking that though made her stomach drop. She shouldn't be feeling anything for him. Cole didn't like her. He didn't want her here. He was marginally civil to her on the best of days.

Except when Annabelle was born. He was different then. And he's treating Brayden better.

That was true too. She saw him teaching Brayden how to saddle a horse the other day. He'd been polite to her when they crossed paths this week at least, but he was distant.

And still not sleeping at home.

"Please, let me set you up," Gabriela's voice pulled her eyes away from Cole's ass resting on the stool now as he talked to Zach. "I think you need to put yourself out there. Get your mind off of, other things." She pointedly looked at Cole. Now Gabriela knew Abby was checking him out, not that she was subtle about it.

"I don't know. What if I'm not here that long? That wouldn't be fair to Dan, would it? That wouldn't be fair to anyone." Abby flicked her eyes towards Cole once more. He was tipping his head back and laughing at something Zach said.

A woman about their age slid on the stool next to Cole and smiled at him. He lit up, hugging her as if they were long-lost friends. It was obvious they were by his reaction. The jealousy hit her hard, catching her off guard. He never laughed with her like that. When Annabelle was born, he showed more emotion, but not the outright howling he was currently engaged in, and he certainly never voluntarily hugged her. Usually, he squirmed away when he was forced next to her, like on the truck ride home last week. He'd practically crawled out of the window so their legs wouldn't touch. Why was she fixated on someone who didn't care? She should go on that date. If anything, it would take her mind off Cole. Who knows, she could have a fabulous time and Dan would end up being her soulmate.

"Fine. If he says he wants to go on a date, I'll go out, but don't make him feel bad. I don't need a pity date. I'm content being single," Abby stated, watching Cole run his fingers through his hair.

Gabriela clapped her hands in excitement, "I'm going to get us more drinks."

She gathered their glasses and headed to the bar. Not wanting to get caught staring at Cole, she fished her phone out of her bag and absentmindedly scrolled. This could be a good thing. She had moved to a new town, left her job, learned new things on a ranch like Muriel wanted. Dating a hot doctor could be the ticket to pushing her fully out of the mundane existence she'd been in for the last five years. If she didn't end up liking Dan, no harm, no foul. It was only one date, what could go wrong?

Emilia Abraham

Chapter Thirteen

Cole

HE'D been talking to Zach for the past fifteen minutes, desperately trying not to look over at the girls' table. He'd seen them when he came in, but he didn't want Abigail to think he'd followed her here, because he hadn't. He was hungry, that was all.

Next to him, was Sandra, a girl he hadn't seen since high school. Brad, her brother, enlisted right after graduation and lived somewhere overseas. He greeted her with a hug but pulled back quickly. She had been friends with Jen, his high school sweetheart, but Sandra didn't bring her up, content to prattle on about Brad living in Japan. Cole hadn't talked to him in almost ten years.

Gabriela walked up, saving him from listening to Sandra

go on about her husband who was cheating on her or, so she thought. He didn't care about her failing marriage, but he didn't know how to end the conversation politely.

"Gabby!" He greeted her as if he didn't know she was going to be here. She didn't look convinced though. "How's it going?" He turned his back on Sandra, hoping she'd take a hint. She didn't.

"Good. Getting another round for us." She gestured back to the booth she and Abigail were at. Abigail was buried in her phone. Did she know he was here? Of course not. She would have left the minute he came in if she knew.

"Mi Amor! Another one for us!" She called to her husband at the other end of the bar. He had slipped away once Sandra sat down, easily escaping, while Cole was stuck. Bastard. Next time they went to the Sun Oak Diner, he was leaving him there to deal with Adam's wife, the gossip, by himself.

Zach came over, stealing a kiss from her. Sometimes it was hard to be around them. He was happy for them, but knowing they had something he thought he would have with Jen, stabbed at an old wound he thought long since healed. He didn't want Sandra to start talking again, so he looked back at Abigail. Her long hair swung forward and covered her face from view. Had she been looking at him? Probably not. He hadn't given her any reason to feel anything towards him but hate. He almost wished he'd done things differently, but it was too late now.

Cole wasn't as convinced as he once was, she scammed Muriel. She was sincere. Authentic. There was no way her joy was fake. There was too much genuineness to her to believe she developed an elaborate scheme to get the ranch. Plus, she mentioned more than a few times she wanted to enjoy the time she spent here. That didn't sound like someone with a plan to take the ranch from him. He was sure the money at the end would help her to, at the very least, buy a new car. She was still leaving though. Abigail might be having fun learning things now, but she'd leave eventually. No one wanted to be stuck in this small ass town. The last thing he should do is get involved with her.

Zach and Gabriela were still talking when he turned his attention back. Anything to take his mind off his roommate in the booth with her sun dress riding up her thighs. Gabriela was going on about something to do with the new doctor

"...I think they'll hit it off. Abby gave me the green light, so I'll ask him tomorrow if he's up for a date. That girl has the worst luck with dating. Can you imagine? A full suit of armor!" Gabriela giggled.

Abigail agreed to a date? His chest ached and he rubbed it absentmindedly. Sandra started blathering again, but Cole didn't register any of her words. Gabriela and Zach were still talking as she gathered the girls' drinks, but he couldn't concentrate on them either.

She was going on a date. Why did that surprise him? She was beautiful, fun, and friendly with everyone. She was the shiny new thing in town everyone wanted to know about. Come to think of it, so was Dan. Cole hadn't met him properly yet, but he'd seen him around town. He looked like a T.V. doctor. Blonde wavy hair, tan, with shiny white teeth he flashed at everyone. He looked charming. Cole bet Dan would charm the pants right off of his girl.

Wait, his girl? Abigail wasn't his. He had no claim to her, other than the one keeping her here to fulfill his Great-aunt's will. There was no reason he should feel jealous of Dan at all. So, they were going on a date. Who cared? They'd hit it off, and start dating. They'd find a little place in town and move in together. Soon Dan would propose at the town gazebo, not that Sun Oak had a gazebo, but Dan would build one for the occasion, because of course he did carpentry on the side. They'd build their house together to live in and have babies and live happily ever after. Like the perfect little couple.

What the hell.

He had to get out of here. He'd created an entire life story that sounded bitter as hell. Ignoring Sandra's attempt to draw him back into conversation he stood up and started for the door. He heard Zach call out to him, asking him where the hell he was going. Dammit, he had ordered food. Whatever, he'd find something at home. Or not. If he ate anything right now, he might throw up. His mind kept circling back, *she's going to fall in love with the doctor.* Because who wouldn't fall for him? No one in their right mind would pick Cole over a doctor.

No, he didn't want Abigail to pick him. He wasn't in the running, and he was perfectly fine with that. He pulled up to the house ten minutes later, deciding it was better this way. It was good she was going on a date with that guy because Cole didn't want to date her. Good for her. He was fine.

He still slammed the door when he went inside though, prowling through the house. It felt so empty now. He loved the solitude before Abigail came along. He loved his own space where no one would intrude. But now, without Abigail, it was too quiet, like a tomb. Was this what it would be like when she finally left? He barely spent any time here with her and still, he could imagine her standing in the kitchen, making her tea in her revolting cow set. It was good she was going on a date. She'd take her tea set with her when she moved in with Perfect Doctor Dan.

Cole made his way to his office. He had taken most of the paperwork he'd been working on to the cottage with him, but there must be something he could do to get his mind off this merry-go-round he was on. Shuffling old receipts from the feed store and notices for past cattle auctions, his fingers caught the edge of an envelope. Cole pulled it out and stared. Muriel's letter. He had forgotten about it in the aftermath of the will and Abigail uprooting his life. Cole collapsed into his chair, fingering the edges of the crumpled envelope. He smoothed out the surface, trying to get rid of the wrinkles.

His heart already heavy, he slipped his finger along the edge and opened it, pulling the letter out. Seeing her handwriting again stabbed at his heart. He missed her. He hadn't allowed himself to grieve yet. She had been such a large part of his life, he felt like she would still be on the other end of the phone if only he would call. She had been the only constant in his life for a long time, without a doubt the only female influence since he was ten. After his mother had taken off, Muriel had stepped up and raised him, giving him no-nonsense advice. She taught him how to cook, how to take care of things, to be himself, how to treat others. Somewhere along the way, he'd lost some of what she'd taught him.

Four months after he lost her, he read the words she had written for him. He thought it would be a lot of advice on keeping the ranch going, continuing the legacy her and Uncle Harlan had bestowed upon him. Perhaps something about how proud she was of him. What he found was not that. Cole didn't know when the tears had started, but they rolled down his face, wetting his shirt.

Muriel, what did you do?

That crafty woman orchestrated everything to bring Abigail to him. This scheme seemed to be in the works long before she changed her will. She wanted him to fall in love. She knew he would never leave the ranch, didn't want him to, but if he wouldn't go to love, she would bring it to him. He sighed as he looked out the window into the night, the letter fluttering to the floor. There was more, but he couldn't see past Muriel's matchmaking. He bent and picked the letter up again, reading the rest.

You're stuck, boy. Not at the ranch, but in life. You have to see yourself as more than that place. You'll never leave, and I know why. It's why Harlan and I built our legacy there, but you're not living and that ain't right. You're the son we couldn't have, but that means I gotta work twice as hard to kick you in the ass when you're being too stubborn. Find someone whose soul lives at Sundown too.

And she thought that someone was Abigail. Cole felt so dense, forgetting Muriel was devious and mischievous at her core. For some reason, after she died, he concocted this image of a sweet, old lady who drank tea all day. But that wasn't Muriel at all. She was stubborn and tough and manipulative. If she couldn't get you to see her way by force, she'd con you into doing things her way. It was laughable now to think Abigail somehow schemed her way into the will. No, this was all Muriel. You couldn't con a con artist.

And now she's going on a date with Perfect Doctor Dan.

He should have read Muriel's letter earlier. They could have avoided a lot of the issues-issues that started and ended with him. Cole shook his head and put the letter back. No, this didn't change anything. He knew Abigail hadn't had a hand in this for a while now. It didn't change the fact she was still going to leave. It didn't change the fact she was going on a date with someone else. It didn't mean anything at all.

Muriel might have thought Abigail was the other half of him, the one to "wake him up", as she put it, but she was wrong. He wasn't meant to share this life with anyone else. Cole had his ranch and his friends and that was all he needed. He thought about being nicer to Abigail, but that would only make things worse in the long run. He would be cordial…or just ignore her. That would be a better plan.

Cole stuffed the letter in the drawer of his desk and slammed it shut. He had to focus on the next few months, keep the ranch running, and survive her leaving. No more hiding at the cottage though. This was his house, and he wasn't going to let her run him out of it. They could coexist in this space and later things would go back to normal after she left. If she stayed, she wouldn't be staying for him, and that was fine. Cole was perfectly fine. He wouldn't want it any other way.

Chapter Fourteen

Abby

ABBY knew she shouldn't be nervous about her date, but she was. She'd been on countless dates, but getting set up was new. The dates she picked for herself, or at least the ones the dating app chose, hadn't exactly been winners, but it was easy to write them off as crazy things that happened and were over. But being set up? What if he collected beanie babies, or only ate his food in alphabetical order or like to lick eyelids? What if she just didn't like him? How could she explain to Gabriela he wore socks with sandals and that was a no-go for her?

There was more pressure. If it didn't work out, he was the only doctor in town. If she broke her ankle running after a goat, she'd have to see him. Awkward. It was easy in the city. Even when she did randomly run into one of her internet dates, she could lose herself in the crowd. Sun Oak was not the place to lose yourself in a crowd. There weren't enough people to *make* a crowd.

But what if he's as perfect as Gabriela says? What if he sweeps you off your feet?

Abby sighed and looked herself over in the mirror one more time. She'd left her hair down, even though she needed a haircut soon. That hadn't been at the top of her list since she got here. She'd put on actual makeup, mostly to cover the dark circles under her eyes. Abby wanted to blame the 5 a.m. wake-up times, but that was wishful thinking.

Abby pulled on the yellow sun dress she'd worn the first day at Sundown. She didn't have many dresses to begin with. She'd left behind all her work attire. No reason to schlep around in pantsuits and blouses in the country. Abby had gotten used to wearing jeans and long sleeves in the heat. Not having to worry about wearing makeup was amazing. She wasn't concerned about what others thought about her. They were all covered in dirt and dust and shit most of the time. Now though, she felt she had to do something to look put together as she slipped her feet into her sandals. She could have put on some heels, but she couldn't be bothered anymore. If this date flopped, she might swear off dating forever. It wasn't like there was anyone else she was interested in.

You're not fooling anyone.

I'm not interested in Cole.

Who said anything about Cole, hmm?

Ugh, the voice in her head was annoying. It sounded a lot like Muriel. From the grave she was poking at Abby, forcing her towards truths she didn't want to see.

I'm going on this date. I'm going to have an amazing time. I'm not going to think about a certain surly rancher who will not be named. That was the best pep talk she could give herself.

Abby tried to be quiet as she went down the stairs, but with flip-flops and wooden stairs, it wasn't an easy task. She hadn't seen Cole around much, even if he was back to sleeping in his room. She still didn't know where he stayed while he was away, but she ignored the questions swirling in her mind about it. It wasn't her business in any case. If anything, he was avoiding her more now. The only glimpses she caught of him were of his back, riding out on Trigger to wherever the cattle were that day. She slowed and started to creep down the stairs, scanning the living room and kitchen. Not seeing him she continued to the front door, gathering her purse along the way. She caught movement out of the corner of her eye and turned, finding Cole filling the door frame of his office. Their eyes met, and they stared at one another, neither moving. He didn't look angry, but he definitely wasn't happy. She waited to see if he would ask her where she was going. Did he know she was going on a date? Did he care?

After what felt like forever, he turned towards his office, closing the door with a soft click. Well, that answered her question. Of course, he didn't care. He apparently didn't register her existence anymore. He hadn't gone out of his way to make her think otherwise. She sighed and went to her car, more determined than ever to leave thoughts of Cole behind.

* * *

The Sun Oak Diner was one of the few places in town to go on a date, which wasn't ideal. It felt like half of the town was here for dinner. Abby knew she wouldn't be able to keep anything from the gossips, but half the people would try to listen in on their conversation and the other half would stop by to chat, but going to Monroe's was not an option. Not only was Zach there, but Cole could show up, and first dates were awkward enough without a potential fiasco.

Abby fidgeted with her purse strap, standing outside the front door. Did she go in? Was he already here? She should go get a table and wait for him to show up. She'd done this a dozen times before, but every time she felt the nerves deep in her stomach. Why did dating have to be so complicated?

She wanted to skip all the awkward parts and settle into 'we like each other and regularly hang out in sweatpants together' phase.

"Abby?" A deep, strong voice rang out behind her. She turned and became 100 times more nervous.

Damn you, Gabriela!

This man wasn't super cute or gorgeous. This man was hot. He was the kind of guy they put in picture frames at the store, complete with a trophy wife and adorable kids, all laughing on a blanket in front of their white picket fence. His golden blonde hair was styled like he had just walked off a magazine cover. His green eyes radiated warmth. Gabriela had overestimated Abby's appeal because there was no way this guy would have agreed to a date with her. She thought she was pretty, but this guy was way out of her league.

Close your mouth Abby, you're drooling, Muriel's voice rang in her head.

Recovering with as much dignity as she could muster, she stuck out her hand to introduce herself. Shit, she hadn't said anything yet. Now he would think she was a crazy person who didn't know words.

Didn't know words?

She wasn't thinking in complete sentences, much less saying them out loud. She was screwed.

"Sorry! Yes, I'm Abby. And you're Dan. The new doctor

in town." Wow, way to not sound like a stalker.

He grinned, showing off perfect, white teeth, as he took her hand, shaking it slowly.

"Yup. I'm the new doctor in town. Good to meet you." At least he hadn't asked if she was crazy. Yet. "Ready to go in? I told Mrs. Swenson to save us a table if it got busy."

She nodded and swung around, almost tripping on nothing as he reached past her to open the door. Great, not only was she tripping over invisible divots in the concrete, but she narrowly missed slamming her head into the door. He caught her elbow and steadied her, flashing her another grin.

He smiled too much. Maybe that was what was wrong with him because there had to be something. No one was this perfect. Ooh, he could secretly be a murderer, like Dexter. Who moved to a small town like this when you looked like him to be the only doctor? She shook her head and smiled in thanks as he pulled back, letting her go in first. She had to get her thoughts under control. There was no reason to think he was a serial killer or kicked kittens for fun.

Inside was packed, but there was one table, smack in the middle of the hubbub with a homemade reserved sign sitting on it. Mrs. Swenson waved from behind the long counter others were sitting at and pointed to the table, smiling widely at them. As they weaved through the other tables, Dan put his hand on the small of her back to guide her through. He must have been afraid she'd crash into someone and fall into their meal. Ordinarily, there was a tingle when a guy pulled that move, but she felt nothing.

Dan pulled out a chair for her, and sat himself, like a real gentleman. She couldn't remember the last time a date opened the door for her, much less pulled out a chair. Where did this guy come from?

"So, do you eat here often?" Dan asked, perusing the menu as if this was fine dining instead of a diner in a town of 1,000 people.

"A couple times a week. I get lunch with Gabriela sometimes. I mostly eat at the ranch though." She looked at the menu, for something to do. She knew what she wanted already. Shit, and now she'd mentioned the ranch, which made her think of Cole. Pushing thoughts of him away, she looked at Dan and asked, "you?"

"Truthfully, I eat here almost every day," he smiled at her, "I've been trying to get the practice up and running, so I haven't had much time to cook myself. My mom made sure I knew how though. She didn't want us boys to starve when we went off to college." He smiled again, putting down his menu as Brayden came to their table.

"Brayden! What are you up to tonight?" Abby asked.

"Hey there Miss Abby," Brayden said, blushing and tucking his head. "I'm helping my parents. One of their servers called in, so they're a little short-staffed. What can I get you guys to drink?"

They ordered and Abby watched Brayden shuffle off to put in their orders.

"He seems like a good kid," Dan commented.

"Oh, he is, a little shy, blushes like crazy, but he's trying very hard at the ranch."

"He works at Sundown too? He must be exhausted. Do you help out around there as well?"

"Yeah, I do some easy things, like feeding the chickens and brushing down the horses. Getting the goats back into their pen." She laughed a little, remembering when she thought she'd killed all the goats.

"Do they get out a lot? That shouldn't be a full-time job, right?" Dan winked at her, an actual wink. And it didn't look creepy when he did it either. It looked like he was flirting with her.

Of course, he's flirting with you, you're on a date silly!

Forcing her attention back to Dan, she launched into the story of almost killing the goats, leaving out the part where Cole yelled at her and told her to learn to knit. She regaled him with other antics from the ranch. It was hard to tell the stories without bringing up Cole. He always popped up whenever something went sideways for her, so while she tried to concentrate on the animals or other ranch hands, Cole was never far from her mind.

She made Dan laugh. A lot. He had a nice laugh, full-bellied and genuine as if he truly thought she was funny. She always thought she was witty, but you never knew if people were trying to be polite or if you were actually funny. Dan talked about moving to Sun Oak, saying he wanted to start his own practice after finishing his residency, and how he had grown up in a small town himself. He told her about his childhood, wanting to be a doctor to help people and some stories from school. As the food arrived, they ate while he asked her questions about herself, where she was from, what she thought of living in a small town versus the city. This was the best date she'd ever been on. As the date wore on, she felt herself relaxing, laughing easily.

This was the kind of date you saw in movies. Dan was nicely dressed, and she was sure he hadn't forgotten his wallet. He didn't try to convert her to veganism or join his MLM business. He didn't talk about how many women he'd slept with and how much hotter they were than her. There was no confession of love or proposals of marriage. Gabriela was right, this man was perfect.

As they finished dessert, he asked, "did you want to get some coffee?"

"Oh, I don't drink coffee. Muriel converted me to tea." And there was the stab at her heart. The older woman was never far from her mind, but sometimes the pain of losing her came out of nowhere. She dabbed her eyes with her napkin, hoping Dan didn't notice. Nothing like crying on a first date to seal the deal.

His gaze was sympathetic, "I've heard about her. She owned Sundown, right?"

"Yes, and gave me half of it for six months, which was not something I expected, but exactly what I needed." Abby didn't want to talk about the debacle Muriel had shoved her into, but he must have heard the gossip. She expected him to ask more questions, but instead, he nodded and changed the subject, asking her about college. Dan paid the bill, despite her offer of paying half, and they walked to her car. Thinking about Muriel had thrown her off. The nerves rose, but something was wrong.

I don't want him to kiss me, she realized. She was on the best first date ever, but she felt almost empty. There was no spark, no butterflies, no desire for it to never end.

"I had a great time," Dan said, stopping by her car door. He smiled at her, but a look of confusion followed. "Is something wrong?"

"Oh, no. No, this was perfect." Abby bit her lip, looking away.

"But?" he prompted.

"Listen, this has been a wonderful date. If we had met a

year ago, I'd be ecstatic, but…" she paused, not wanting to have this talk. She'd never had to let someone down before.

"But you're not ready," Dan finished for her.

"No, it's not that. This has nothing to do with you." Awesome, she was giving him the 'it's not you, it's me speech'. "I just…I think I'm…well…" How the hell did she say she wanted someone else?

That was what this was truly about. She wanted Cole. She was falling for him, despite all his gruff and assholish ways. There was no reason she should, he was rude to her and didn't want her, and couldn't spend two minutes in her company before he was glaring, but her heart didn't care. There was something behind all those walls he built that she'd caught a glimpse of and her heart wouldn't let it go until she broke them down or was completely heartbroken.

Abby sighed, "I think I'm hung up on someone else and it wouldn't be fair to you if we dated while I couldn't completely be invested."

She stared at his shoulder, not wanting to meet his eyes. When she couldn't take it anymore, she looked at him. He was smiling, no longer flirting, but with understanding.

"It's Cole, isn't it?" he asked knowingly.

"Is it that obvious?" She asked, biting her lip again. This was the weirdest way to end a date, talking about another guy.

"No, but listening to you tonight, you were holding back whenever you talked about the ranch. At first, I thought it was because you two didn't get along, but now? Well, let's say it makes more sense. You're great Abby. If he doesn't see that he's either blind or dumb. Or both," he chuckled.

"Yeah, well, I don't think I'll be making any progress with him, but thank you. I did have a great time though."

"Good. Friends? This small of a town, I'd rather be friends than try to run to the other side of the street when we cross paths." He laughed and opened his arms for a hug.

"Friends for sure." She hugged him back before he opened the door for her to slide in.

"Goodnight Abby. Good luck with everything." He smiled again and shut the door, strolling away down the sidewalk.

"Goodnight," she whispered after him, hoping she hadn't made a huge mistake.

Chapter Fifteen
Cole

COLE glanced at the clock on the mantle, sitting below the television. It was only 9 p.m., but Abigail had been gone for over two hours. He tried to keep working in his office, but thoughts of her kept intruding. Was she having a good time? Was he treating her well? What if she didn't come home tonight? He shook his head and took another drink. He'd poured himself a whiskey shortly after she'd left, planning on making himself something to eat, but instead, he was nursing this drink still.

Cole rolled the ice cubes he kept having to replenish around his glass and checked the time again. Two minutes since the last time he'd looked. He tried to talk himself into going to his bedroom, but couldn't move. He kept thinking about why he cared so much about her going on a date. Muriel's words kept echoing in his head.

You're stuck.

He sighed. She was right, he was stuck. His past relationships had been excuses to push others away. If he didn't let them in, it wouldn't hurt when they left. He never wanted to leave the ranch, but at some point, he let go of the dream of sharing it with someone else. Now he was forced to share it, and he had pushed her away too. Right into Perfect Doctor Dan's arms.

Where would Perfect Doctor Dan take Abigail on a first date? The diner, or Monroe's, since those were the only places with food in town. Cole would have taken her someplace quieter than the diner. A Saturday night in town, the place would be packed with locals. Every gossip in town would be trying to listen in on them.

Cole would have brought her some place on the ranch; gotten her up on a horse. She'd been talking about learning to ride since she got here. That would be the perfect date. Saddle up Lucy and Trigger, pack a picnic, and visit Annabelle. Watch the sun set over the fields. Lay back and watch the stars come out. They'd talk. The goats would wander in because that was his luck. One of them would trample through their picnic as he went in for a kiss. And she'd laugh because she wouldn't care about something being perfect, only that it was real.

Perfect Doctor Dan could never do something like that. He probably didn't open the door for her. Most likely made her pay for her meal. A guy who looked like that would only talk about himself. He wouldn't try to get to know Abigail. He'd talk about how amazing he was because he was a doctor and make her feel like less because she was working on a ranch. Dan obviously had malpractice suits coming out his ass, which was why he had to open his own practice in a small town. No one was going to look into those things here.

She must be having a good time though since it was coming up to 9:15 now. What could they possibly be doing that was taking this long? Were they still eating dinner, walking down Main Street? Or had someone interrupted them? Gabriela set them up, so Abigail would talk to her after. Girls did that; talked about a date. She was just spilling how Perfect Doctor Dan wasn't so perfect. He probably tried to get her back to his place and Abigail wasn't that kind of girl. What a douche, treating her like shit the whole night and then trying to get laid. Headlights cut across the front windows.

Finally!

Not that Cole was waiting for her. He was taking advantage of his own living room not being taken over by another person. It wasn't creepy he was here. He lived here.

He owned this house and didn't have to explain why he was sitting here, drinking, with a single lamp on and nothing to do.

Cole heard the front door open but didn't turn around. He hadn't said anything to her before, but she had looked amazing. She'd worn the same dress as when she'd tried to kill his goats. She'd put on makeup, though, but that shouldn't have been as surprising as it was. Whatever she'd done had made her eyes bigger, but he liked it when he could see the freckles sprinkled across her nose. There were more of them now that she spent most of her day in the sun.

Cole knew the exact moment she saw him since she left out a soft, oh. He could sit here and pretend she wasn't there, pretend she hadn't come back from a date, pretend she had been in her room the whole night. Ignore her like he had been for weeks, but he was sick of ignoring her. He was sick of trying to get her out of his mind. He was sick of being stuck.

"How was your date?" Cole asked, looking at the watered-down whiskey. He hadn't decided to say anything, but the question popped out. He wanted to sound casual like he didn't care, but his voice was gruff.

"Oh, uh, it was fine," Abigail said faintly from the entryway.

"Yeah? Where'd you go?" Why was he asking her questions? This was not what he wanted to talk about. He wanted to know if she had thought of him at all tonight. Had he occupied her mind like she had invaded his?

"We went to the diner. It was packed. Seemed like the whole town was out tonight." She was blatantly trying to change the subject, but for some reason, he couldn't let it go.

"What'd you have to eat?" Not the question he wanted to ask.

"A club sandwich, why?"

"Did you get dessert?"

"Yes, I had some rhubarb pie, since I have a feeling you'll ask," she said in an exasperated tone.

"Did he pay?" Still not what he wanted to know.

"Um, yes?" She said it like a question instead of an answer. Perfect Doctor Dan could have pulled the 'forgot my wallet' trick.

"Huh. Did he kiss you?" He stared down at the liquor, still swirling it around the glass in his hand. He didn't want to know, but he couldn't stop himself. It was better than asking if she was going to see him again. Then again, maybe not.

"What?" Confusion rang through her voice, still echoing from the entryway.

"Pretty simple question. Did he kiss you?" He set his glass down on the table.

"Why do you want to know?" Why was she avoiding answering was the better question. Cole stood up, stepping around the chair to prowl towards her.

"Did he kiss you, Abigail?" As he came closer her eyes darted around, eventually settling on his.

"That is none of your business." Her chin came up, defiance set on her face. Cole's hands came up on either side of her head, leaning against the front door, caging her in.

"Answer. The. Question. Abigail." He leaned down. Her breath had grown shallow and her blue eyes dilated as she stared into his. She was holding something back. Her body's response to how close he was wasn't fear, it was desire. He wouldn't make that move though. He wasn't going to kiss her unless she made it clear she wanted him to. It was obvious Perfect Doctor Dan hadn't kissed her. But why?

"Was it because you didn't want him to?" he asked carefully.

"Why wouldn't I want him to?" Abigail whispered back, her eyes darting down to his lips and back up. She was biting her lip again. She had to know what that did to him.

"Because you know he can't kiss you like you need," he whispered back.

"How do I need to be kissed?"

"Like this." Cole leaned in little by little. If she didn't want this, she had plenty of time to say no, duck under his arm, and run to her room. Instead, she licked her bottom lip, her eyes flicked back to his, and started to flutter shut.

Fuck it.

He grabbed the back of her neck, slamming his lips into hers. She tensed for a second, before she melted into him, her hands gripping his shirt. He licked her bottom lip, wanting her to open for him, groaning as she did. Their tongues dueled, never seeming to get enough. Cole pulled back slightly, sliding the hand on her neck to cup the side of her face. He nipped at her lip, soothing it with his tongue after. His other hand ran down her side and settled on her hip, his body pushing hers back into the door. He eased back a little more and kissed her slowly, thoroughly. He couldn't get enough. Her hair, tickling his cheek and her distinct scent filled his nose with her sweet aroma. Her hands flattened against his chest and moved towards his shoulders as if to pull him closer.

I could kiss this woman forever.

A thud walloped on the door at Abigail's back as something crashed into it. A muffled bleat came through. Cole and Abigail sprung apart, both gasping. The goats had gotten out again. Abigail looked like she was going to laugh, but her eyes caught his and the beginning of her smile faded. He didn't have time to hide what he was feeling and it was all over his face, he was sure.

Shock, confusion, and guilt. Cole hadn't meant to kiss her. He had, but not really. He shouldn't have kissed her at all, and certainly not like that-basically mauling her. He didn't know what to do. Cole hadn't kissed anyone in a very long time. Any time he spent with a woman; he didn't kiss them at all. It was too personal, too intimate. He should have stayed in his room. Hell, he should have stayed at the cottage. He had to get away. With the way she was looking at him, she would try to talk about what just happened. She opened her mouth, but he stopped her.

"No. This was a mistake. Just…no." He spun around and practically ran to the French doors in the living room that led out to the back porch. He had to leave; go anywhere other than back in there with her. If he did, he didn't know what he would do or what words might come out. He couldn't see her again tonight, maybe not even tomorrow. Not after kissing her like that.

Chapter Sixteen

Abby

Cole's words echoed through her head. She was exhausted, not sleepy or tired but utterly drained. The day felt like it would never end. She was frozen after Cole dropped his bomb on her. Abby thought it was funny, getting interrupted by the goats again. Instead, it was a wake-up call for Cole.

This was a mistake.

Did he mean kissing her? Her being here? Going along with Muriel's crazy will? Or her? Was she the mistake? There wasn't another explanation. She'd seen the look in his eyes. Shock and confusion, but also something else. Guilt. He looked horrified after kissing her. It wasn't a look you wanted someone to have after such passion. As if that wasn't a low enough blow to her confidence, he had run.

Straight out the door, to his truck, and off down the driveway going god knows where. Bastard. He couldn't get away fast enough. After admitting to herself, she had feelings for him, one kiss had sent him running for the hills. Oh god, and she had told Dan. She admitted to him, out loud, she was hung up on Cole. Why did she have to open her stupid freaking mouth?

Abby was raging now. She stomped up the steps to her room and slammed the door. She opened it and slammed it again for good measure. It was a good thing he ran because she was liable to throat punch him if she saw him right now. Who did that to someone? Who badgered them about their date with another guy and then kissed the shit out of them? Who ran away after like his ass was on fire? An asshole, that's who.

As she stood there, seething, she surveyed her room. She wanted to throw something. She wanted to kick the door and rip all the sheets off her bed and wreck everything, if only so her room would match the chaotic thoughts raging in her skull. Abby marched to her bed, ripped a throw pillow off it, spun around, and chucked it against her closet door with a shriek.

It didn't help. She stared at the pillow laying on the floor and all the anger drained out of her. She sank on the bed, grabbed another pillow, and hugged it to her chest, Her fingers absentmindedly tracing the embroidered flowers on it. Why did he run away?

Was there something wrong with her? She always assumed her bad luck with dating had more to do with the internet and the guys who frequented dating sites, rather than something with her, but for all she knew she was missing something. Something broken within her. Dan said he had a good time, but he mentioned something was off. She thought it was her realizing she had feelings for Cole, but maybe Dan had seized her words and used them to not have the awkward conversation himself. It was his way of letting her down easy. Could something be wrong with *her*? Something she'd never seen before?

Cole hadn't let her down easy. On the drive back to the ranch she had resolved to bide her time and leave when the six months were up. She never imagined Cole feeling anything other than contempt for her, but when he started asking if Dan paid for the meal, as if he was worried her date hadn't treated her right, she thought he cared for her well-being beneath his gruff exterior and was falling for her too. What a stupid dream.

He made it clear he didn't like her. Attraction didn't equal love. She knew that. She didn't think she was in love with Cole, but she knew it was more than wanting him in her bed. Based on his response, it was not the case for him. He wanted her body, not her heart. A tear fell, splashing on to her hand, still gripping the pillow. Sighing, she threw it back on the bed and grabbed the other pillow, tossing it next to its mate. Methodically, she got ready for bed. Determined to get it out of her system, this burning ache in her chest.

She'd take five minutes to mourn what had never been in her grasp in the first place, and after, she'd go to sleep. Cole didn't deserve more than five minutes of her tears.

A blaring ringtone startled her out of sleep two hours later. She grabbed her phone from the nightstand and squinted at the screen. 11:37 p.m. Who the hell was calling her this late from a number she didn't know?

"Hello?" she answered groggily. She spent at least twenty minutes instead of five, lamenting her descent into singledom and her eyes itched from the tears.

"Abby girl!" Zach's voice rang out. "I don't know what you did to this guy, but I'm going to need you to come get him. He's had a little too much to drink and I'm not letting him drive."

Abby could hear the music from the bar, along with raucous laughter in the background. Zach was practically yelling into the phone.

"What are you talking about Zach? Come get who?" He

couldn't be talking about Cole. In the three months she'd known him, she'd never seen him have more than one or two whiskeys. A drunk Cole would be a disaster. The noise from Zach's end became muffled as she tried to pick out anything from the background noise.

"Sorry, it's a madhouse in here tonight. We got some douchey frat boys passing through. Locals are pissed. Can you come get Cole?" He sounded distracted.

"Oh, uh, sure. I didn't realize he went out." Abby started shuffling around, looking for the clothes she wore earlier that she hadn't bothered to put away.

"Sure, you didn't. Listen, I'm not going to get all into your business but you got him tied up in knots girl. He was ranting and raving. Then practically crying in his beer over everything that happened tonight. I don't know what's going on between you two, but you should sit down and talk. Like a real talk. But not tonight, 'cause he's, well, wasted."

"Well, why'd you serve him so much if he was like that?!"

First, she had the most awkward ending to a date, then she got interrogated and passionately kissed, and now she had that same guy run away and go get drunk, and she was the one at fault here? And she had to go pick his stupid ass up and drag him home. She put the phone on speaker and tossed it on the bed, so she could pull her dress on and slip on her shoes.

"Sorry, Abby." At least Zach had the decency to sound remorseful. "I'm not blaming you. He's been a big asshole to you. He's beating himself up over a lot of things though. I think meeting you stirred up a lot of feelings he thought he buried deep down. He hasn't had the easiest life. Please give him a chance to explain. Don't let him off the hook, but let him get it out, ya know?"

"Yeah, okay. I'll think about it. I'm getting in my car now. Be there in ten. Try to get a glass of water in him." Abby sighed as she grabbed her purse.

"See you soon. Thanks, Abby."

When she pulled up to the bar ten minutes later, she could barely find a parking spot. Zach wasn't kidding when he said it was crazy busy. Even for a normal Saturday night, this was insane. People were milling about out front, cars parked all along Main Street and filling up the small parking lot to the side of the bar. Abby waved to a few people she recognized from around town but beelined for the door, intent on getting Cole out of here. She hadn't thought about the fact almost everyone she knew would be seeing her. She hadn't brushed her hair and her makeup was probably smudged. Thank god she'd had the sense to change out of her pajamas.

Abby pushed past a group that was congregating in front

of the door propped open with a brick, and stopped as she stepped inside, scanning the space. Cole would be parked on one of the stools at the bar, but with her height, she couldn't see him. A gap in the crowd opened up and there he was, right at the end, waving his hands frantically at Zach, who had a bemused look on his face. She waved, trying to get Zach's attention. He lifted his hand, motioning her forward.

A large group moved in front of her, headed for the pool table. Suddenly it was like half the bar emptied out, thank god. Maybe she could get Cole out of here without any trouble. It was loud enough she couldn't hear herself think. Intent on getting to Cole she didn't register the other man's voice until a hand wrapped around her upper arm and yanked her backward.

"Hey! I was talkin' to you gorgeous. Where you running off to?" A preppy boy, no older than 22 or 23 had a grip on her arm and was slurring his words. There were two other guys behind him at the table she had passed moments ago. They all were in Bermuda shorts and polos, with all the buttons undone.

He gave her a little shake, and she was jolted out of her shock. She tried to pull her arm free, but as drunk as he was, he had a tight grip. Abby looked up at him, he couldn't be more than 5'8" but those four inches he had on her were still intimidating.

"Let go of me." She tried to sound firm, but there was a tremor in her voice.

Preppy Boy threw his head back and guffawed. His hair was cut and styled to within an inch of its life, brushing the back of his popped collar. Did kids pop their collars anymore? Seriously. Now she was getting pissed. She had a shit night and these asshats weren't making it any better.

"Come on sweetheart, we're just looking for something pretty to look at. Why don't you come join us? We'll get you a drink and you can loosen up a little." Preppy Boy started to tug her towards their table.

"Let go of me now. I don't want a drink. I want you to leave me alone." Usually, she'd be worried about pissing off a drunk guy, but she didn't care anymore. With the crowd, the smart thing would be to let her go about her business instead of harassing her, but he didn't, go figure. She tugged, trying to pull back but her current footwear had not been a good choice for resisting an overly eager frat boy.

"She told you to leave her alone," Cole's voice cut through the noise of the bar. Preppy Boy looked back, squinting at Cole as his two friends stood up. They weren't quite as short as their ringleader; Cole would still tower over both of them, but it would be three on one. Not great odds.

Uh oh. She peered over her shoulder at Cole as the two guys brushed past her and Preppy Boy, who was still gripping her arm tightly. She tried to twist free, but he yanked her towards him so her back was to his chest and grabbed her other arm. This was not good. The two came at Cole, trying to intimidate him, but he glared back, waiting for them to make their move. She could see Zach at the bar, on the phone with the sheriff most likely.

"Ooh, this is going to be fun, isn't it sweetheart." Preppy Boy was talking right into her ear. Naturally, he thought he was whispering, but he was close to shouting. She tried to put distance between their bodies, but he held her with an iron grip. What the hell did this guy do to have that tight of a grasp when he wasn't getting drunk and manhandling girls at a bar. Cole shifted his gaze to her, watching her struggle to get away from the asshole. He shifted his stare to the guy behind her. She had never understood the saying 'if looks could kill' before, but she got it now.

Without warning, the man on the right threw a punch towards Cole's face, trying to catch him off guard. Cole ducked and sucker-punched him, and he went down like the sack of shit he was, but as Cole turned to the one on the left, he swayed a little. These frat boys weren't the only ones on this side of drunk. Cole had been here for two hours, because of her. She didn't think it was her fault he ran away and was halfway along to three sheets to the wind, but she was the reason he was standing where he was now. Defending her from drunk boys who didn't know how consent worked.

"Sure you wanna do this?" Cole voice was steady, but his eyes were glassy, and he was listing to the side.

"Why don't you mind your own fucking business huh? She's with us."

"Oh no, son, she's mine." Cole took a swing at him but the frat boy must not have been as gone as the other two, because he dodged it. She wasn't sure how used to bar fights Cole was, but was holding his own as the two circled each other. She'd never been in a fight, and after this one, she hoped to never be in one again.

With Cole's back turned, Preppy Boy got it in his head that was a perfect time to start edging her towards the door. Why he wanted to go through all this trouble, she didn't know, but she wasn't going anywhere with him. She wiggled and pulled her arms, getting her right one out of his hold but his hand gripped the back of her neck, forcing her head to her chest, and she yelped.

"Knock it off bitch," he said through gritted teeth. Preppy Boy grabbed a fistful of hair and wrenched her head back, making her yelp again.

Cole whipped towards her, having heard her cry of pain. Abby's eye's widened as she watched the frat boy behind him grab a beer bottle off a nearby table. She tried to shout out a warning, but Preppy Boy twisted his fist in her hair tighter, making her wince instead.

Abby watched in slow motion as the bottle smashed into the back of Cole's head. His eyes rolled up into his skull, and he slumped to the floor. She yelled Cole's name before she stomped on Preppy Boys' foot. He cursed and his grip relaxed a little. She was able to pull her free arm back and smash her elbow into his stomach. As his hand fell from her hair she turned around and kneed him as hard as she could in the balls.

God please, never let him have kids now.

She turned back as Zach vaulted over the bar towards the last one standing. He tackled him to the floor as the sheriff and a deputy came through the doorway, surveyed the scene and took out some handcuffs.

"Well, Zach? Which ones we takin' in?" he asked, as if five men sprawled across the bar floor, two of which were out cold, was nothing new.

The deputy looked at the back of Cole's bleeding head and turned to her, "better get him to Doc, Miss Abby," she said. Abby had never met the deputy, but the woman clearly knew who Abby was.

The sheriff cuffed the guy Zach was sitting on and the bartender grabbed some water. Cole sputtered as he opened his eyes, his entire face dripping from the pitcher Zach dumped on him.

"Better get up and start walking. Abby girl can't carry your ass to Doc's place," Zach grinned at him. Cole just blinked back blearily.

"Huh?"

Well, this was going to be fun. Zach helped him up and steadied him while Cole found his feet. Abby was talking to the deputy, but she could see Zach muttering something to Cole. It would be a miracle if he got out of this without a concussion.

Somehow Abby was able to guide Cole out of the bar and two blocks down to Doctor Dan's place. It was pure luck he lived in the apartment above his office, or she would have never known where to find him. As she knocked, she wondered how awkward this conversation would be. Three hours ago, she ended a date and told him her hang-ups about Cole and now she brought Cole to him to patch up. The door swung open and Dan stood there with sleep pants and no shirt on, looking shocked.

"Well, hello there Doctor Dan." Cole narrowed his eyes at the doctor. Abby smacked him and turned back to the confused man.

"Sorry, we have a bit of an issue which requires a doctor. And you're the only one in town." She smiled sheepishly at him. If she wasn't worried about Cole's head, she would have driven him the half-hour to Woodbury to the clinic there instead of having to endure this awkward encounter.

"Oh, sure. Why don't you go down to the front and I'll let you in, get you guys checked out." Dan shut the door as they turned back to the stairs. Going up the stairs had been brutal, going down them she hoped he didn't miss a step because there was no way she was catching him.

A good five minutes later, Dan lead them back to the only exam room. The space was small but clean. There wasn't much more than the four rooms and some closets tucked away, but for such a small town they didn't need a lot. Gabriela said Dan made a lot of house calls like they used to back in the day. It made sense in a town this size with so many farms and ranches around.

"So, what happened?" He washed his hands as Abby started to tell him the bare minimum. She didn't want to go into the whole story, since she wasn't *that* injured, all things considered. Plus, she was embarrassed by the whole thing.

"There were some drunk kids who wanted a fight and one of them hit Cole over the head with a beer bottle. He fainted…"

"I didn't faint," Cole groused, "and they weren't some drunk kids. They were assholes who wouldn't take no for an answer." Dan raised his eyebrow at them.

"Sit down and let him look at your head," she said exasperated. He sat but glared at Dan. "And stop looking at him like that, he's going to help your stubborn ass, so be nice," she added.

He didn't say anything, but he had the decency to look embarrassed. The doctor didn't comment, as he pulled on some gloves and moved to look at Cole's wound. It wasn't deep and had stopped bleeding, but he winced when the doctor started digging around.

"Did the bottle break?" he asked.

"No. But his eyes rolled back in his head, and he keeled right over," she answered.

"You make it sound like I didn't hold my own before that," Cole grumbled. She could tell he was going to be a terrible patient.

"Well, you don't need stitches, but you could have a concussion. Hard to tell since you've been drinking, but it's a safe bet with this kind of wound. You'll have to be monitored for 24-hours to make sure it doesn't get worse though. Pain killers for the headache I'm sure you'll feel tomorrow and lots of water. No strenuous activity, like ranch work. No reading, phones, or television until the headache goes away without pain meds," Dan washed the cut as he went through everything, "Abby, if he's more disoriented, starts slurring his words, has blurry vision, or starts vomiting call me right away."

At least a whole day stuck to Cole's side? She was sure

he'd just love that.

"Look at her arms Doc," Cole said, holding the gauze Dan gave him for his head, nodding towards her. She crossed her arms, trying to cover the bruises starting to form.

"What's wrong with your arms?" Dan asked, coming around the bed to her.

"Nothing is wrong with my arms," she glared at Cole, begging him to keep silent.

"A guy grabbed her. Wouldn't let go. Had a good grip on her. Got bruises." Cole hung his head, suddenly looking tired.

"Let me take a look. I'm sure it's nothing, but it doesn't hurt to check them out." Dan took her wrist and rotated it to see the dark outlines of Preppy Boys' hands on her upper arms. She winced when he pressed on them lightly.

"Looks like some bad bruising, ice might help. It's a good thing Cole was there to help get you away from him." Dan grabbed a clipboard and started writing, while Cole started to chuckle.

"I didn't get her away from anything. She stomped on his foot, elbowed him in the stomach, and kneed him in the balls." Cole started to laugh harder.

"Well, guess you can take care of yourself huh?" Dan grinned at her, but she didn't notice. How did Cole know all that? Dammit Zach. She stared at Cole, who caught her eye and laughed harder.

"Is he okay?" she asked, afraid of the answer.

Dan chuckled along with Cole, who clutched his stomach as his peals of laughter filled the small space.

"Most likely the adrenaline from everything. Or it could be he liked seeing you beat up another guy." He winked at her, looking at Cole before turning back to his paperwork. She didn't bother telling Doc that Cole had been out cold when she'd gotten away from the guy. She was too tired. This day felt like it was lasting a lifetime.

They left shortly after, making their way back to her car. Cole had calmed down some, only occasionally giggling. The sheriff's car pulled up to the Doc's as they were leaving, yanking the frat boy Cole had knocked out and Preppy Boy out of the back. The sheriff called out to them for Abby to come write a statement when she got around to it.

As soon as Cole saw Preppy Boy though, he lost it again. His peals of laughter echoed down the now quiet streets. This time, Abby couldn't help but join in. They must have looked crazy or drunk, stumbling down the road, snickering the entire way.

Chapter Seventeen

Cole

GROANING, Cole grabbed his pounding head. He was in bed, but couldn't remember how he got there. He cracked his eyes open and looked at the clock seeing it was after 4 a.m. before closing his eyes again with another groan, memories of rushing out of the house, away from Abigail filling his mind. Cole remembered getting to the bar. The night was a haze after that. Flashes of memories that didn't make sense popped behind his lids. The back of his head felt like it was on fire and the inside felt like tiny miners had taken up residence.

Squinting he glanced to the side and saw Abigail shuffling by his bed. What was she doing in here? He opened his eyes wide and looked around, trying not to move. The chair in the corner of his room had one of those hideous throw pillows Muriel had left behind and the Afghan blanket Abigail brought with her when she moved in.

Looking back at her, he saw her mess with something on his bedside table. He cleared his throat and tried to say something, but his words got caught. He tried to swallow but his mouth was too dry. She turned to him holding a glass of water.

"Hey, I got some pain meds here. I'll help you sit up so you can take them." She tucked her arm under his shoulder, and he slumped back against the headboard. She handed him the glass and some pills and waited, tapping her foot. He shook his head and instantly regretted it. Pain radiated down his head and into his neck. Cole swallowed the meds, handing the glass back to her when it was drained.

"What happened?" His voice sounded like gravel. Had he hit his head falling off the stool? He remembered drinking a lot more than he normally would, but not much else.

"You don't remember anything?" Abigail bit her lip, looking away.

"I remember…I remember getting to the bar. They're some snippets of other things, but they don't make sense." He avoided mentioning why he fled in the first place. The last thing he wanted to do was have that conversation now.

"Oh. Well, do you remember drinking like a fish? Or

talking to Zach?" she asked, narrowing her eyes. What the hell had he done to warrant that look?

"Yeah, I remember that." He tucked his chin to his chest, avoiding her eyes.

"Do you remember getting into a bar fight and getting bashed over the head with a beer bottle? Hmm?" Oh, she was angry for sure.

"What?!" His head snapped up. Wrong thing to do as more pain radiated from the back of his head. He pressed his fingers into his temples and winced.

"And do you remember me lugging your drunk concussed ass down the street for Doc to check you out?"

"Uh, not really."

"And do you remember laughing hysterically like a psychopath all the way from Doc's until you got home? That wasn't mildly alarming whatsoever," she drawled out and started arranging the things on his nightstand, moving them around, avoiding his eyes.

Cole's eyes fell shut once more. When she mentioned the laughing, the memories came rushing back to him. Drinking and ranting to Zach about Abigail and how screwed he was. Seeing that douchebag grab her. Cole confused why she was there and then seeing red at the dick manhandling her. His two friends coming at Cole. Punching them. Her yelp echoed in his mind. Pain and waking up to a pitcher full of water in his face. Zach telling him Abby kicked the guy's ass. Her taking him to the Doc and losing it when he imagined this tiny woman kicking the shit out of the guy. And then seeing the sheriff hauling them into Doctor Dan and losing it again with Abigail joining in.

He couldn't help it. He started chuckling, his shoulders shaking. It hurt, but the laughter bubbled up out of him. Damn, Cole wished he could have seen her in action. Abigail must be a force to be reckoned with when she decided enough was enough. He laughed harder when he thought of Douchey cupping his balls when he had climbed out of the cruiser.

"It's not funny," she said, fighting a smile.

"Honey, imagining you kneeing Douchey in the balls and knowing he had to go to the doctor to make sure he could still reproduce is the funniest shit I've ever seen," he quipped. She glanced away, but he caught her smile turning into a full-on grin.

She cleared her throat, "well, you should get some more sleep. You'll heal faster that way, and your hangover won't be as bad." She started to walk back to the chair, clearly intent on curling back up.

"Why the hell are you sleeping in a chair?"

"Doc said you have to be monitored for 24-hours, in case you start throwing up or something." He was glad she wasn't calling him Dan anymore. Doc was impersonal.

"But why are you sleeping in a chair?"

"Well, I'm not going to sleep on the floor." She was back to being exasperated with him.

"Sleep in the bed." Now that he was awake, he wasn't going to make her uncomfortable just to take care of him. She kept messing with her blanket, her back to him.

"I can't go to my bed. I have to make sure you don't die in the middle of the night."

"This bed. There's enough room. It's a king-size bed." He started to slide down, swallowing a groan when his body protested the movement, as she twisted around to him.

"I can't share a bed with you." He saw her eyes bug out, staring at the other side of his bed like it would swallow her whole. He rolled his eyes and sighed.

"Honey, just get in the bed." He settled down and closed his eyes, hoping she'd listen for once.

"I'm fine in the chair. I don't want you to throw up on me." She was protesting, but she hadn't sat, still clutching her blanket in her hands, twisting it back and forth and biting her lip.

"I'm not going to throw up on you. Get in the bed Abigail." He closed his eyes again, suddenly exhausted. The room had started to spin. Cole heard her sigh as she shuffled to the other side. He felt the mattress dip slightly as she crawled under the sheets.

"Fine, but only because I'm getting a crick in my neck. If you throw up on me, I'll let the goats in your room." She sighed as she settled on the pillow to the left of him.

Cole fell asleep with a smile on his face, despite the pounding behind his eyes.

* * *

Cole woke sluggishly, pulling the warm body next to him tighter against his chest. A feeling of contentedness spread through him. Eyes still closed he sucked in a deep breath, Abigail's scent filling his lungs. Slowly, he blinked open his eyes and peered down at the woman fast asleep next to him, his arm circling her waist. She was tucked up to him on her side, her back nestled into his chest. He watched her steady breaths, mouth slightly open, chest rising and falling. Her freckles stood out from her barely tanned skin as sunlight streamed through the gap in the curtains. Her makeup was smudged, but it made him feel like he was seeing the real Abigail. He'd seen her in pajamas and work clothes and dressed up; with and without makeup; hair up and down and messy and styled, but this right here was the most beautiful he'd ever seen her.

They could start over. This could be their new beginning.

Would Abigail want to start over? Could he convince her to give him a chance? Cole wanted her to see him as more than the gruff asshole she'd seen since she got here. He could be more. He could give more. He didn't have to be stuck.

She's still leaving.

He closed his eyes, trying to block out the voice. Was it worth it to try something different? He'd been in this rut for so long, keeping the ranch going, pushing others away, that he didn't know if he could change. If she left, after he put himself out there, he knew he would close himself off more than he ever had before. He would bury himself in the ranch and everyone would move on around him. Hell, his only close friend had been married for four years. They'd start having kids soon, and he-he would be alone. Alone with his ranch. No one to share it with. No one to pass it on to. The end of a legacy.

That will happen if you don't try.

It would. Now that Muriel had planted the seed of more, he had to try, and let it grow. He thought he was fine before, but she was right, he wasn't living. He was maintaining. Now that he could admit he felt something for Abigail, he owed it to Muriel, to himself, to at least try, see if she was willing to look for something more with him. He hoped he hadn't missed his chance after her date with Doctor Dan. She could say she wasn't interested in Cole, and she wanted to pursue things with the doctor. Hell, *he'd* pick Perfect Doctor Dan over himself any day. Especially after how he'd treated Abigail. But he would make it up to her if she gave him a chance.

Abigail shifted in her sleep, wiggling closer and sighing. Cole laid next to her, not moving, enjoying this moment. He tried to empty his mind of what would happen when she woke, tried to relish the feeling of hope blooming in his chest. She shifted again, yawning and stretching. Cole kept his eyes closed, not wanting her to know he was watching her while she slept. He'd pretend he was still asleep and see what she would do. If she pulled away, she wasn't on the same page as him yet. He'd try to get her there though when all was said and done.

He knew she was awake now, laying with him, but she eased from his arms and out of the bed. Disappointment crashed through him. He forced himself to pretend to sleep, not wanting to face her now he knew they were on opposite ends of where he wanted to be. Abigail left the room, quietly closing the door behind her.

He rolled over on his back, wincing slightly. His head still hurt and now his chest ached too. Staring at the ceiling while the sunbeams waved across it, he tried to think of something he could do, something he could say that would convince her he was going to do things the right way from now on.

You could start with an 'I'm sorry'.

That was exactly what he needed to do. And a 'thank you' for taking care of him. Then another apology. He'd say sorry every day for the rest of his life if she'd let him in. Cole could explain to her why he had these walls built up. He could tell her about Jen and his mama, and they could talk about Muriel. Abigail deserved to know more about his great-aunt when she was younger and running the ranch. She was what brought them together in the first place. She was the connection they had. If Abigail didn't want this thing, whatever it was, to go anywhere, she at least deserved to talk to him about Muriel.

Resolved, he sat up stiffly, suppressing a groan. He couldn't tell if his head hurt because of the concussion or hangover, but he needed more pain meds. Pulling back to sit against the headboard, he looked to his nightstand. Abigail had given him pills last night, but they weren't there. Just an empty glass. Sighing, he rested his head back, trying to gather the energy to search his medicine cabinet and get in the shower. Before he could though, his bedroom door opened again.

Rolling his head to the side he saw Abigail standing there. She'd changed into her pajamas, the shorts mocked him. She was also holding a tray of food. Dammit, she made him breakfast. His face split into a wide grin. He met her eyes, and she smiled back uncertainly, so he patted the bed next to him.

"Hey, I didn't want to wake you if you were still sleeping, but I figured you might be hungry. I don't know when you ate last. I made some eggs and toast and bacon. I don't think you're supposed to drink coffee, but I got some orange juice and water, so you can take more meds for your head." She tentatively went to the bed, setting the tray next to him. "Oh, and I called Diego and told him you were sick. I didn't know if you wanted him to know what happened, so I said you were sick, and he'd have to take over anything urgent and to push back everything that wasn't. I hope that's okay."

She was rambling and it was the most adorable thing he'd ever seen. And she was blushing. And biting her lip. He still couldn't stop grinning at her. She'd come back.

"Good morning," he said, picking up the tray and putting it on his lap.

"Oh, good morning." Her blush deepened as he washed down the pills with some juice.

"Where's your food?" He hadn't started eating yet, just kept smiling at her.

"I was going to eat downstairs. It's fine." She looked towards the door and back to him, eyes fixed on the food in front of him.

"You're going to make me eat alone?"

"Um, I guess so. Unless you want me to eat with you?" Her lip slipped back between her teeth. She looked hopeful, at least he wanted it to be hopeful.

"Go get your food, Abigail. We need to talk." Well, that didn't come out like he'd hoped. His grin faded, and he stared at his food, but not before catching her face fall into a frown. He opened his mouth to fix things, but she turned and was halfway down the hall before any words came out.

Shit, now he really needed to apologize.

Chapter Eighteen
Abby

ABBY gathered food on her plate. She wasn't hungry anymore, but she should go back with something in her hands. At least it would keep her busy while he flambéed her heart. She thought he was offering for her to join him because he wanted her to, not so they could talk. Hot and cold. First, he was grinning, like something changed last night between them, and now he was dropping the bomb on her of a 'talk'. She knew things wouldn't magically be better because they got in a bar fight together, but she thought it might be a new start.

Sighing she gathered up her tray and started towards the stairs. If Cole didn't want anything to do with her, she would still have to live here, but she could stay out of his way. He had enough practice with avoiding her, maybe she should have taken notes. She could spend more time in town, instead of helping out at the ranch. She didn't know if she could keep hanging around if he was here too. Not after admitting to herself she had feelings for him.

Abby needed to figure out what she would do come October. She was putting it off, subconsciously not wanting to leave, because six months wasn't long enough to know if she was out of her rut. She didn't want to go back to her boring job, staring at a computer all day, tucked away in a cubicle, or back to dating apps and disappointment. She didn't want to go back to the city at all. Where she would end up though, was up in the air. Abby could use this time to research where she belonged, what she wanted to do with her life, now Muriel had forced her to clear the fog from her mind.

But she couldn't do it here. Before she might have been able to stay, even without owning half of Sundown. But with where things stood with Cole and how she felt about him, she couldn't see him and still move on. She couldn't watch him meet someone else and fall in love and live the life she might have had. Not that she knew what she wanted, but she'd be perpetually stuck in neutral, waiting to see if there was something between them.

She hesitated in the doorway. Cole was looking at his

phone. Wait…he was looking at his phone!

"No!" She wanted to dash into the room and knock his phone out of his hand, but she was carrying a tray and the glass of juice she'd poured wobbled. His head popped up in alarm.

"Are you okay?" His look of concern looked genuine.

"You're not supposed to be on your phone!" She hurried as fast as she could, setting the tray on the nightstand between the door and the bed. Leaning across towards him, she plucked his phone from his slack fingers. He watched her with concern, but then grinned.

"Ooo-kay." Damn him and his mercurial temperament. Couldn't he either hate her or love her? Dammit, no.

Stop thinking about him falling in love with you.

She set his phone on her tray and picked it all up, turning to sit on the chair. It wouldn't be particularly easy to eat there, but the only other place was the bed, next to him. It was one thing to share a bed in the middle of the night when everyone was tired; completely different to share it in the light of day when all the awkwardness took front and center.

"Over here, Abigail. You won't be able to eat sitting there." Cole picked up his fork and started to eat his eggs. They had to be cold by now, but he kept shoveling them into his mouth.

She did an about-face, almost losing her glass again. Cole

grabbed it and set it next to his. He grabbed her tray, nodding his chin at the space next to him. She sat, keeping almost two feet between them, making him lean over to set her tray on her lap.

"I'm sorry," Cole said in between bites of rubbery eggs.

"Excuse me?" She couldn't have heard him right.

"Eat before it gets any colder." He pointed his fork towards her food, waiting for her to pick her own up before he turned back. "I said I'm sorry."

"For what?" There were a million things he could be apologizing for.

"A lot of things." He kept focused on his food, not looking at her at all. "Eat."

She grabbed her fork and started to eat some eggs, but immediately stopped, coughing a little while trying to swallow the mouthful she had. Cold eggs were the worst. How Cole ate the first bite, much less the whole pile she'd given him, was beyond her. She grabbed some bacon instead, waiting for him to elaborate, but he stayed quiet, plowing through his food. Silence descended between them, and she didn't know how to respond. She didn't want to say it was okay, because that was what she always said. Someone said they were sorry, she said 'okay', even if it wasn't.

"And thank you." Cole took a huge bite of toast, still not looking at her.

"You're welcome."

Silence again. This was so awkward. She ate a little faster, hoping to escape this room. He sounded like a robot, saying those things because he was supposed to, not because he meant it. Cole sighed and set down his fork still clutched in his hand, though he'd long since finished his eggs. She could feel him looking at her, but she kept her focus on her food.

"Thank you," he said again.

"You said that already."

"I know. But I mean it. Thank you for taking care of me. Last night was…well, I typically don't drink that much. Or get in bar fights."

"Or get walloped with a beer bottle?"

"Or get walloped with a beer bottle," he agreed, moving his tray to the floor, and handing her juice over. She'd forgotten it was there. He leaned back again closing his eyes.

"Does your head still hurt?" she asked gently.

"Yeah. I'd like to lie and say it isn't bad, but it feels like a full marching band is doing a parade in here," he said, tapping his temple.

"Do you have blurry vision? Do you feel like you're going to puke? You're not slurring your words…disoriented! That was the other thing." The last thing she needed was him to have a brain bleed or something. If he died, did she have to take the whole ranch? She couldn't run this place without him.

He grinned, though his eyes were closed. "Nope. Other than a hangover headache from hell and a tender head I'd say I'm fine."

"Okay then." She felt foolish. She had to get out of this room before she started rambling.

"Are you done?" He was looking at her now, holding his hands out for her tray.

"I've got it. I'll take them downstairs and clean up. You should get some rest." She tried to pick up her tray and scootch across the bed, but instead, he pulled it from her hands, leaning down and stacking her tray on his. She winced, thinking of the grease seeping into the wooden bottom. Whatever, they were his trays, she wouldn't have to deal with them.

"We need to talk." The seriousness of his tone made her freeze. She would sit here and listen, and after she would run. He obviously needed to get this off his chest.

"Abigail."

She stared at the comforter by her hip, tracing the dark swirls in the gray fabric.

"Abigail, look at me." Timidly she lifted her head.

"I'm sorry." A glint of sadness flashed in his eyes.

"You already said that," she whispered.

"I'm sorry I didn't give you a chance. I'm sorry I blamed you for Muriel's will. I'm sorry I ignored you. I'm sorry I was an asshole. I need you to know I'm sorry. I shouldn't have taken all my anger out on you when none of it was your fault. I'm sorry." He leaned back again, closing his eyes.

"You blamed me for Muriel's will?"

"Oh, yeah," he groaned lightly, "I thought you were a con artist who took advantage of a helpless old lady to get her money."

"Um, are we talking about the same person? Muriel was the furthest thing from being a helpless old lady," she giggled, imagining Muriel playing bingo at the VFW.

Cole joined in, "somehow, she morphed into the typical old grandmother type in my head after she died. Drinking tea and sending birthday cards with five dollars in it to kids and knitting by the fireside."

"Is that why you told me to learn how to knit?!" It would make more sense than if he thought she looked like someone who *would* learn to knit.

"What's wrong with knitting? It's a good skill to have. I've heard it's very relaxing." He smirked at her, and she smacked his arm and smiled back, but swiftly turned away.

Shit, shit, shit.

She had no defenses with him when he was smiling and joking. It was too easy to think things were going to be okay, but she'd seen him turn into Mr. Asshole at the drop of a hat.

"Don't do that," Cole rumbled, his hand brushing hers.

"Don't do what?"

"Don't freeze me out." He hooked his pinky with hers.

"Like you do?" She stared at their linked fingers, her stomach a ball of nerves, and her head a chaotic mess. What the hell was happening here?

"Precisely. I've been stuck for so long, freezing people out, thinking it'd be better that way, but Muriel was right. That's not a way to live." He sighed but didn't let go of her hand.

"What do you mean Muriel was right?" Is that what was in his letter? She had reread hers so many times over the past few months, the creases were worn. Abby could recite the whole thing from memory. She wondered what Cole's said, but that wasn't something she could ask, especially someone whose demeanor continually changed.

"Yeah. She said I was stuck. Not at the ranch, but in life. And she was right. I've known for a while you weren't scamming me, but I was still freezing you out."

"Why?" She leaned back against the headboard too, resting her head to see him better.

"A conversation for another time." Abby knew she couldn't push him. He had opened up more in the last ten minutes than he had the entire time she'd known him.

"Okay," she tried to pull her finger away to get the plates, but he laced the rest of his fingers with hers.

"I mean it. We'll talk about it later when my head doesn't feel like an anvil got dropped on it. I don't want to keep doing things like we were. Or like I was, I guess."

He watched their hands, his thumb rubbing hers. Abby felt like she had whiplash though. Her thoughts had been so out of control since yesterday. A half-hour ago she thought about leaving, imagining him not wanting her here. Now she didn't know what he wanted. She was scared though, terrified to put herself out there, fearing the rejection. If she did, and he rebuffed her, where did that leave them? Where did that leave her?

"Do you want to start over?" The nerves rang through in his voice. It was like he had looked inside her head and asked the one question she was afraid to.

"I'd like that." Relief washed through her, making her entire body sag.

He shifted to face her, pulling away. He smiled, stuck out his hand and said, "Hi, I'm Cole."

She mirrored him, slipping her small hand into his warm grip. "Hi Cole, I'm Abby."

"Nope, I think I'll call you Abigail." He was beaming at her, hope shining through. It was a completely different man sitting in front of her, but not. She'd caught glimpses of him before. It was those glimpses that intrigued her. It was why she started to feel like there was more to him than what he presented to the world.

"Abigail is fine. But you'll be the only one to call me that." She smiled, feeling lighter than she had since she'd come to Sundown Ranch. But holy shit he was blushing. Honest to goodness blushing. She didn't know it would show with how tan he was, but there it was, reddening his cheeks, while he still smiled and kept a hold of her hand.

"Good. I'd rather not share you."

"Good thing I'm not a glass of milk."

What? What the hell did that mean? A glass of milk? Milk wasn't something people shared. Mortified, she felt her own cheeks reddening as she tried to pull her hand free, but he held on, tipped his head back, and laughed.

"Why the hell are you laughing?! It didn't even make any sense!"

Cole kept going, struggling to take a breath. He was still chuckling, but he groaned. He let go of her hand and massaged his temples. Great, now she broke him. Cradling his head in his hands, he peered at her through his fingers, joy still dancing on his face.

"Honey, this is going to be so much fun."

* * *

* * *

Five days later and Abby was going to kill him. Cole was the worst patient ever. The first two days were fine. He slept, ate, and slept some more. Then the third day hit, and he wanted to get back to work. Forget that his head was still aching, and he could hardly wash his hair by himself. Forget that sunlight made him wince. Forget that he fell asleep ten minutes after eating. Nope, he wanted to get back to the ranch.

"Get back in here," Abby called from the dining table, where she was trying to make sense of the supply order. She still wasn't letting him on the computer, or his phone, or letting him watch television. She'd talked to Dan, and he said it should be fine. But every time Cole looked at a screen he would squint and grimace until she turned it off. And then the grumbling would start.

"I want to sit on the porch," Cole called back from the entryway.

"No, you don't. You want to try to catch Diego so you can get an update and go tearing off to solve all the minor, insignificant problems that have come up, knowing full well Diego has everything under control."

Why are we getting 17 bags of chicken feed this week?

"Abigail, I've been running Sundown for over a decade. I've worked through sleet and flooding…"

"…and hail and random freezing and drought. Yes Cole, I know. And you'll go back to work in two to nine days when you're not liable to keel over and die." They'd had this conversation several times a day for the past three days.

"What about the supply run?"

This was his latest tactic. He wanted to go into town to get the order from the feed store by himself because he'd "been driving for 15 years and was perfectly capable". Like hell she was going to let him get behind the wheel. He would be distracted by a bird, hit a bunny, and crash his truck into the ditch. His concentration levels weren't entirely at full strength either.

"I'm going to get supplies after I talk to Diego. But lucky you, you get to come with!" She looked over her shoulder and gave him a cheeky grin. He was still in the foyer, holding on to the door handle like he could sneak out without her seeing.

Suspicion clouded his face, "why do you think I'm going with you?"

"To prevent you from driving me batshit crazy," she mumbled, turning back to her paperwork. In reality, it was because he had a check-up with the doctor, but she wasn't going to tell him before she had to. Every time she mentioned Dan, Cole would mutter something, but she could never make it out. She tried not to bring Doctor Dan up.

"Fine. What are you doing?" Cole abandoned his escape attempt and sat next to her.

"I'm checking the supply order." She wanted to be able to do this on her own. She wanted to prove to Cole she was capable of taking care of things around here for him.

But 17 bags of chicken feed?! Did they need that many? For a week?!

"We don't need 17 bags of chicken feed," Cole said as he leaned over, looking at the paperwork.

"I know." She didn't. "I don't know who ordered that much." It was Cole.

"It's a misprint or something. I'll tell Adam we only need seven. I'm sure he can sell the rest at the store."

"No, I'll tell Adam, because I'm getting the supply order. You'll stay in the truck, in the passengers' seat. The entire time. When I get there. When I go in. And when we're loading it all up." Abby leveled him with a stern look.

"Abigail, honestly, I feel fine. Stop being a…" he stopped; his eyes widened while hers narrowed.

"A what Cole?"

"Nothing. But I'm fine." He glanced away, looking horrified.

"No, what were you going to say? A nagging harpy? A scolding shrew?" She didn't care about his concussion; she was going to put him six feet under herself. Her eyebrow cocked, "a bitch?"

"A mothering hen! I was going to say, stop being a mothering hen. Seriously, woman, I don't think you're a bitch."

"If you did what the doctor told you to do, I wouldn't have to mother you, now would I?"

Cole rolled his eyes and muttered under his breath again.

"What was that?" she asked sweetly.

"Nothing." Cole laid his head down on the table. It was only lunchtime, but he looked exhausted.

"Why don't you go lay down? I'm going to make lunch when I'm done with this."

"I'm not tired," his voice was muffled, but he still sounded petulant.

A knock on the door saved her from replying. Whatever her response would have been, it wouldn't have been kind. Cole didn't bother to lift his head as Abby pulled open the door and stepped out to join Diego on the porch, pulling the door closed behind her.

"What's wrong Diego." It wasn't a question, Diego was usually smiling, but his lips were pulled down.

Diego swiped his ball cap from his head and ran his tan fingers through his dark hair. He looked off towards the barns and pens, though he couldn't see them from where they stood. Great, he was stalling. This had to be bad.

"It's Betsy and Annabelle." Diego returned his gaze to her, concern in his brown eyes.

"What about them?"

"They're not doing well." Diego looked at his feet, crushing his hat in his hands.

But they were fine. Abby had seen them yesterday. Diego said they were fine. How could they not be fine? Suddenly Cole's arm snaked around her waist, pulling her back into his chest, giving her strength. She hadn't even heard him open the door.

"What happened Diego," Cole used his boss voice. The one that demanded answers and results. Diego exhaled, glancing at Abby again before his gaze rested on Cole.

"Looks like an attack. A cougar or wolf," he paused, undoubtedly not wanting to be the one to give this news in front of her. "We think Betsy was trying to protect Annabelle. Calf has some wounds on her."

"How bad is it?" Abby asked, tears welling in her eyes.

"It's bad, Miss Abby. Real bad. Betsy doesn't look like she'll make it. And with Mama gone, well…"

A sob rose up in Abby, choking out of her. Watching Betsy give birth had been life-changing. Experiencing it with Cole had been almost magical. She turned into Cole's chest and soaked his shirt with her tears. It wasn't fair. Cole's arms wrapped around her, holding her while she wept.

Chapter Nineteen

Cole

"YOU ready?" Cole asked as they stood outside the barn holding his hand out to her. They hadn't talked about what they were to each other. With him being injured and her trying to pick up the slack, it didn't seem like the right time. Abigail's eyes were still glassy when she hesitated before she nodded, taking his hand. It was cooler in the dark space. More workers were milling around than normal too. Cole could hear Betsy's distressed cries echoing in the space, mixed with Annabelle's frightened bleating. She gripped Cole's hand tighter as he pulled her along, and he squeezed her hand in response, trying to give her comfort.

The stall was lit up, Betsy laying on her side, blood darkening her black coat. She had gashes down her sides and her legs were shredded. Abigail turned away, a whimper escaping her as Cole tucked his arms around her shoulders, pulling her into him. He could hear Annabelle in the next stall, crying out.

"Why aren't they together? They should be in here together," Abigail scolded him, dragging in a heavy breath and looking towards Annabelle's stall.

"We keep them separated so the calf doesn't injure the cow more," Cole explained.

"Annabelle won't hurt her. They need to see each other. She needs to know her baby is okay!" Cole stopped her from trying to rush out the stall to get the calf herself.

"Okay, Honey. It's okay. Brayden will get her in here."

Cole pulled her back to him, nodding his head at the kid, who had a worried look on his face, but did what Cole asked. As soon as Annabelle was led in, she went straight to Betsy, laying down next to her, and they both quieted. Betsy started to lick Annabelle's head, calming down.

"Well, guess we didn't have to worry about that and now they're together. The vet will be here soon." Cole looked at Abigail, "what do you want to do?" She was absorbed in watching the pair comfort each other, so she didn't look like she heard him.

"The vet?" she asked after a beat.

"Yeah, the vet will come and check them both out; see if

there's anything we can do."

"I want to stay." Conviction filled her voice. He knew she would want to, giving the cows any comfort she could.

"Okay, we'll stay." Cole tugged her gently towards the wall, the same one they had sat against when Betsy had given birth. Abigail leaned back; eyes drifting shut.

"I'm sorry," Abigail broke the silence between them, dragging her face on her sleeves, trying to wipe away the wetness.

"Don't be sorry Honey, I know how important they are to you," he answered.

It was never something he wanted to happen, losing one of his cattle, but this was part of ranch life. It was rare, but not unheard of for one of them to run across a predator, but he hated seeing how hard this was on Abigail. She had a connection with these two. They were special to her. He knew Betsy wouldn't make it; her injuries were too much. If Annabelle died too, he didn't know how Abigail would take the loss. When the vet arrived, Cole shook her hand and let her get to work. Abigail started to cry when the vet asked if they wanted to put her down instead of waiting for the inevitable.

"I think we'll deal with it ourselves, thanks," Cole answered, watching Abigail. He settled her back against the wall and walked the doctor out.

"What about Annabelle?" she asked when he sat back down next to her.

"She'll be fine. None of her injuries are severe. Betsy saved her life." He smiled softly at her.

"But she'll die, won't she? Without Betsy, she'll die too, and none of this will have mattered."

"I'll do everything I can to make sure that doesn't happen. But it matters. Everything matters." Cole tucked his arm around her shoulder and kissed her head. They sat like that as the workers filtered out to their own homes for the night.

"Boss, you want me to stick around?" Diego asked as he leaned against the stall door.

"Nah, we're good. Thanks, Diego." Abigail's head was resting on his shoulder now. She had fallen asleep ten minutes ago.

"Funny how that worked out huh?" Diego gave him a sly smile.

"Go home, Diego. Pick up the supply order on your way, and bring it in tomorrow, please." He wasn't going to give Diego any more gossip to spread around town. He didn't care if townsfolk talked about him, but he didn't want them gossiping about Abigail. Unless Diego was willing to talk to Perfect Doctor Dan and tell him to back off, Cole would fully support him running his mouth then.

"Alright, Boss. See you tomorrow," he left, chuckling as he went.

Cole jolted awake hours later, Abigail still leaning on his shoulder. Betsy's tail lashed back and forth and Annabelle was bleating softly, standing next to her mother. Shit, this was it.

"Abigail," Cole said quietly into her hair, "wake up Honey." She moaned while gradually sitting up. The sound sent a shock through him, settling right down south, which was not the time.

"What happened?" she asked, yawning.

"I thought you might wanna talk to Betsy one more time." Gratitude glimmered in her eyes as she looked at him, before glancing at Betsy. Cole moved her closer, staying away from the cow's legs that were twitching and kicking slightly.

"Hey, girl. I am so proud of you. You kept your baby safe…" Cole left her to say her goodbyes, going out the stall door and to the bathroom. Muriel had fought his dad tooth and nail to get it added to the barn, saying she didn't want to step in some workers' pee when she was out here. He finished and looked in the mirror seeing his eyes had dark circles underneath. Sleeping in the barn was never fun, especially when recovering from a concussion. His head hurt, but he didn't want to leave Abigail to get any pain meds.

Cole hurried back to them, stepping inside. Abigail was

still whispering to Betsy, petting her head when the cow wasn't jerking it back and forth. He hoped the cow wouldn't nip at her, but Betsy didn't seem to have enough energy left.

Betsy took one more gasp, her eyes streaming, and she was gone. Abigail kept talking, tears rolling down her face. Annabelle started bleating and pushing her head into her mother's. It was the most heartbreaking thing he had ever seen. He felt like he was intruding, standing here. He had seen plenty of cattle die, but it had never been like this. The agony on Abigail's face was painful for him. He went and gathered her in his arms, holding her.

"It isn't fair," she wept.

"No, it isn't."

* * *

Cole assumed Abigail would sleep in the next morning. It was 2 a.m. by the time he got her to leave and carried her to bed. He went back and put Annabelle back in her own stall and tried to feed her, but she wouldn't eat. It was close to 4 a.m. by the time he fell into bed, his head pounding with each heartbeat. A knock at his door roused him from sleep. Glancing at the clock he saw it was only 8 a.m. Four hours of sleep was not enough. He groaned before he got up and opened the door.

"Hey." Abigail's face was still blotchy from all the crying she had done yesterday. "Sorry to wake you. I need you downstairs." She turned to walk away, but he grabbed her arm and pulled her into him. She shuddered and wrapped her arms around his waist.

"You okay?" he asked, resting his chin on the top of her head.

"Yeah. I want to check on Annabelle. But we need to go downstairs first." She pulled back out of his arms, staring at his naked chest. "Maybe put a shirt on…" she glanced down at his boxer briefs, "and some pants." Her cheeks reddened as she turned around and walked down the hall.

Chuckling he got dressed in jeans and a t-shirt and followed her. If she was up and dressed to go see Annabelle he might as well get going too. He hoped he could fit in a nap later. Maybe Abigail would join him. His face split into a grin as he went down the stairs, but it quickly morphed into a frown when he saw who was standing in the foyer, talking to his woman.

Don't get ahead of yourself. She's not yours yet Cole.

The voice in his head was getting more annoying.

"What can I do for you, Doctor Dan." He looked at Abigail, who waggled her eyebrows at him. He was pretty sure she knew he had a secret nickname for the good doctor, but he wasn't going to tell her.

"Cole! Good to see you up and about." Dan smiled. Was that a dig because the last time he'd been falling down drunk? "I wanted to come by to check out your progress. Abby was going to bring you in for a check-up yesterday but said you had some farm stuff come up."

"Ranch," Abigail said under her breath.

"What?" Dan asked. Well, well, well Perfect Doctor Dan wasn't so perfect after all. Cole brought his hand up to cover his smirk.

"It's not farm stuff. It's ranch stuff." She shook her head, looking at Cole with a glare. Dan still looked confused though.

"I'm fine," Cole said, bringing the subject back around.

"He's not fine." Abigail was still glaring.

"I am fine. She thinks I'm not fine, but I'm fine."

The doctor glanced back and forth between the two, a dawning look of realization crosses his face.

Yup, that's right Doc, she's not interested anymore.

"He squints when he's in sunlight or on his phone. He gets tired after he eats, or walks, or takes a shower. He winces when he moves his head too fast. And he's not sleeping." Abigail listed off his ailments. He thought he had hidden it better, but she had been watching him closer than he realized.

"Well, that's all normal. Keep taking meds and see how it

goes. If they don't clear up in a week, come into the office, and we'll see what more we need to do. In the meantime, Cole, you should listen to Abby. It's obvious she cares." Surprise flitted across Cole's face.

What just happened? He watched as Dan turned to Abigail, smirking, and he winked at her. What had they been talking about when Cole interrupted them? Abigail nodded her head at the doc, smiling broadly.

She turned to Cole and stated, "that's right. Listen to me, because I'm smart."

Dan laughed, squeezing her arm, and turned to go. There was a comfortability between them. Perfect Doctor Dan was flirting with her, right in front of him. Cole glared at the back of his head until Abigail smacked him in the arm. Her look said, 'be nice', so he rearranged his features into a bland smile. She rolled her eyes and sent the doctor on his way with a wave.

That's right Perfect Doctor Dan. She stays here with me. I mean, not 'with me' with me, but essentially, with me.

He was getting another headache.

"You two seemed cozy," Cole said grumpily, heading into the kitchen. Abigail's hand shot out and grabbed the mug he had put under the coffeemaker before he could start it.

"No coffee. I'll make you some tea." She went to put a kettle on the stove instead.

"I don't want tea." He sounded like a petulant child, but he was still trying to figure out where Doctor Dan stood in all this. It felt like he was standing right between them.

"Tea is good for you. I'll put honey in it."

"Honey doesn't make it better Honey," he snickered.

"Hardeehar." She rolled her eyes and continued with boiling the water.

"Don't think I didn't notice you avoiding the question, Abigail." As much as he wanted to let it go and pretend Perfect Doctor Dan didn't matter, he did. Cole needed to know where he stood in all this.

"You didn't ask a question, Boss."

Leaning against the counter he watched her pull some fruit from the fridge and the toaster out of the cupboard. He'd tried to help before, but knew she would shoo him away. She wanted a question; he'd give her one.

"Fine. What's with you and Perfect Doctor Dan?" He held his breath, waiting for the answer.

"HA! I knew it!" She turned, pointing a spoon at him, triumph clear on her face.

"Not an answer, Abigail," Cole scowled at her.

"I knew it! I knew it! I knew it!" She was flipping the spoon at him, droplets of water splashing on the floor. He crossed his arms and waited. She wouldn't get out of answering. Now that he asked, he needed to know. He wasn't going to be strung along hoping she'd pick him. It was hard enough to put himself out there in the first place. He had no desire to pursue someone who wasn't going to put in 100%. Plus, he knew what it was like to be played. He couldn't do it again.

"I knew you called him *Perfect Doctor Dan.*" Her sarcasm was on point. She grinned at him, not caring she hadn't answered his question. Cole tucked his chin to his chest, blowing out a breath. Fine, if she didn't want to say, he'd bow out.

"Okay." He turned and walked around the large island. He'd go take a shower and then see if Diego had dealt with Betsy yet. How quickly things could change, last night he was holding her, comforting her, and today he was walking away. Jen taught him he couldn't compete with another man; he wouldn't do it with Abigail too.

"Hey! Where are you going?! I thought we were talking?" He was halfway up the staircase when he turned back. Still holding the spoon, Abigail's hands were planted on her denim-covered hips. Her white shirt pulled across her chest and her hair cascading down her back, she looked like she belonged here. Ready for a day of chasing after goats and cattle. Too bad that wasn't the case.

"I'm going to take a shower. Pretty sure we're done talking." Her mouth fell open, and he bounded up the stairs, taking them two at a time, as his head throbbed with each step. He couldn't face her right now.

Closing the door to the bathroom he leaned against the counter, hanging his head. He couldn't keep doing this. The back and forth of his emotions was exhausting. He said he wanted to start over, but he knew he hadn't made it clear he wanted to date her. He thought he could let his actions speak for him. Either way, he couldn't go on this way, knowing she was apparently going to date Perfect Doctor Dan. He should stop calling him that, but he wouldn't.

Cole pulled off his shirt, leaning over to turn on the shower when the door burst open.

"What the hell asshole!" Abigail fumed. Framing the doorway, hands on her hips, she glared at him. "We were talking and you ran away! Who does that?"

"We weren't talking. I was talking and you were laughing at me," Cole said, facing the shower and putting his hand under the spray.

"I was not laughing at you! God, you can be so frustrating sometimes."

"I can be frustrating? You're frustrating as hell woman!" Fine, if she wanted a fight, he'd fight. Then he'd figure out what the hell was going on.

"I am not! You're the one walking away all the damn time! If you stopped for two seconds and asked a question instead of assuming you know everything, maybe we could land somewhere other than in the middle of another fight!"

"I did ask you a question! And you conveniently didn't answer. I may walk away, but at least I answer a direct question when you ask Abigail."

"Well, now I don't remember what the question was." She was lying. She knew exactly what he'd asked, but once again she was avoiding it.

"Convenient." He twisted around, staring at the shower, waiting for her to leave.

"Fine! I do. I remember what you asked. But you blindsided me." When he glanced over his shoulder, she was staring at her feet, hands now twisting together. Here it comes-the letdown.

She sighed, "we're friends." He snorted. "We are, I mean, I guess. I haven't seen him other than when you were hurt. And it was awkward." At least she was talking.

"Because I was there?" Perfect, now he was getting in their way.

"No, it wasn't because of you. I mean it was, but it wasn't." She ran her hands through her hair, exasperated.

He sighed, "it's fine Abigail. Why don't you go see Annabelle? I'll see you later." He stood there, waiting for her to leave. He couldn't get in the shower with her in the doorway, and she was blocking the way.

She threw up her hands, "see?! You're doing it again! Shutting down and freezing me out!"

"Well, what the hell am I supposed to do?! I can't read your mind, Abigail!"

"It's embarrassing!" She buried her face in her hands.

"What's embarrassing?!" They were both yelling now.

"Everything! The whole thing is embarrassing! The date was fine. It was great and then it wasn't! I got to the end and I just…I just…"

"You just what?!" Cole knew continuing to yell wasn't helping, but he wanted her to spit it out.

"There was the date and the drunk asshole and you got hurt and I had to see Dan again, right after I gave him the 'it's not you, it's me' speech okay! But it wasn't because of me, it was because of you! And he guessed it was because of you and it's mortifying! And now he knows and now you know, oh god, now you know."

She buried her face in her hands again, trying to hide the blush staining her cheeks. Cole had never been happier she was a rambling mess when nervous. She had feelings for him. And she had for a while. Since before her date if she realized it while she was *on* it. And she broke things off with Perfect Doctor Dan because of him. She chose him before she knew he was even an option.

Cole smirked as he stalked towards her. Abigail's head

shot up as he neared, and he backed her into the hallway, pinning her with his body against the wall. His hands came up and circled her waist.

"So, you kind of like me huh," Cole said with a smile.

Breathlessly she answered, "kind of."

"I'm the only one you want, aren't I?" He leaned in and nipped lightly at her earlobe, causing a shudder to run through her body.

"Yes," she whispered.

"And you're mine, aren't you Abigail." He ran his lips along her jaw line, causing her head to tip back before he followed the path back to her ear. "Aren't you Abigail?"

He sucked her earlobe into his mouth and bit it. She moaned in response, her hands coming up and gripping his shoulders, nails digging into his skin.

"I need an answer Honey," he growled, releasing the sensitive flesh from his teeth.

"Yes," she hissed, drawing him closer.

"Good."

Cole grasped her chin, pulling her face to his, crashing their lips together. Need and desire and want coursed through him, forcing him to deepen the kiss, to lap at her lips and plunge his tongue into her mouth. His hand tightened at her waist briefly, before he skimmed it up her side, her shirt riding up and giving him access to her soft skin.

She was passion and warmth and light-everything he had been missing. His mouth left hers, trailing along her jaw, both hands roving up and down her body now. He couldn't get enough of this woman. He made his way down to the pulse in her neck, nipping and soothing it with a kiss as she moaned and sighed for him. Cole snaked his hands around her, grabbing her ass and picking her up, legs wrapping around his waist, rolling against him. He rocked into her warm center as his mouth covered hers again, as her hands gripped his shoulders tightly, pulling him further into her body.

Distantly he heard a whistle, but ignored it. Nothing could pull him away from the woman in his arms. He had fantasized about this moment for weeks; months. He wasn't going to stop unless she said to, or he was inside her.

Suddenly she yanked back, banging her head against the wall hard.

She winced, "shit. Shit, shit, shit."

"Goddammit, what now?" he snapped.

"Put me down! Shit, put me down!" She was wiggling against him, which wasn't helping, but he set her down, stepping away. She yanked her shirt down and turned to scamper down the hall.

Dammit.

Abruptly, she turned and ran back to him, standing on

her tiptoes. Instinctively, his hands wrapped around her waist to steady her. She grabbed his face and pulled him down to kiss him hard. She fled again, yelling over her shoulder, "THE TEA!" And she was gone.

Chapter Twenty

Abby

SHE was staring at his lips again. Cole was off talking to Diego, but for the last several hours she couldn't keep her eyes off him. He glanced over at her, and she bit her lip making him smirk, eyes twinkling, before he turned back to his foreman.

"Miss Abby? Are you okay?" Abby turned back to Brayden who looked at her with concern.

"Yes, I'm fine. Why?"

"You're blushin' real bad, Miss Abby." Brayden pointed out, looking from her to Cole and back again.

"Oh, well, it's hot in here," she said lamely, looking around the barn. Annabelle was crying in her stall, refusing to eat and it broke her heart. She tried to keep her eyes away from Cole as he made his way to them, but she felt herself flush more every time they skimmed over him. This wasn't the time to be fantasizing about Cole.

"Honey, we wanna see if Annabelle will take her feedings from you," he said, looking towards where the calf was. He had been calling her 'Honey' since he came down from his shower earlier. Diego gave him a side-eye the first time, and she caught him nudging Cole when she walked away.

"I've never done that before."

"It's not hard, more frustrating if they don't take it right away. Come on, I'll show you how." He led her in, grabbing a bottle from the table. Cole handed it over and crouched down near the door while he waved her forward.

"You're going to have to get closer Honey. Hold the bottle out, tip it down a bit and see if she takes it. Be careful though, she'll be pulling on it hard if she does."

Abby approached Annabelle slowly. She didn't want to frighten her, so she started murmuring to the calf. Before, it was easy to talk to her, but now, she was a little self-conscious. Annabelle mooed and shuffled towards her.

"Hey baby, you hungry?" She held up the bottle, but Annabelle didn't look interested. "Come on, sweetheart, you need to eat." She held it closer to the calf's mouth, tipping the nipple down. Annabelle looked at her and sniffed the bottle. Abruptly, she latched on and pulled, hard.

"Holy shit," Cole said under his breath. "Hold on tight Abigail. She hasn't eaten in a while, so she'll try to suck it down fast."

Abby held on with both hands, trying not to drop the bottle. Her face must have been pure joy, because when she peered over her shoulder, Cole was beaming at her. After the calf finished, she wanted to stay with Annabelle, but Cole had other ideas. He led her to the horse barn and started saddling Lucy up.

"Cole, you're not supposed to be working."

And I'm going to fall off the horse, she silently added.

"This isn't working, this is riding. And I'm not going to be doing anything, you are." Oh no. He thought now was the best time to teach her how to ride?

"We should wait until your headaches are gone. And Annabelle is settled. And we've dealt with Betsy," she breathed out heavily. Some ranch hands had moved the cow by the time they came this morning, but Abby didn't know where. What did you do with a cow who died? Bury it?

"I don't have a headache, Annabelle isn't going anywhere, and we've already dealt with Betsy." Cole pulled the strap under Lucy's belly tighter and buckled it.

"What do you mean you 'dealt with Betsy'?"

Horror spread through her. Did they slaughter her? Was she going to be eating Betsy for dinner? Abby knew this was a cattle ranch, and she had no problem eating steak, but thinking about eating her cow-it was too much.

"The less you know the better at this point Honey," he said, leveling her with a look. Oh god, they had butchered her. Abby wrapped her arms around her waist, nausea turning her stomach. Cole looked on in alarm, going to wrap his arms around her.

"I don't want to eat Betsy!" she cried as she smashed her face into his chest, trying not to sound like the hysterical mess she was.

Cole's chest rumbled and his shoulders began to shake. She looked up. He was trying to hide a smile and suppress his laughter.

"It's not funny!" She pushed away from him, but he caught her hands in his. Still chuckling, but trying to wipe his face blank, he failed miserably. She narrowed her eyes, hurt.

"It's not. Oh, Honey, it's definitely not. We're not going to eat Betsy. Sometimes we do, but I certainly wouldn't make you go through that. I promise. There are some parts of running a cattle ranch I don't want you to see right now. Later, when it's not a cow you bonded with, sure. But let's say she's being useful."

He said later-as if there would *be* a later. Like he was going to start teaching her about the ranch. Realization dawned on her this was why he wanted to her on a horse. He wanted to show her he was genuine about not going back to being an asshole. That he wanted her here along with a new start. Thank god they weren't eating Betsy though.

"So, we're not going to bury her?"

Alarm flitted across his face. "Uh, no. It's not easy to bury a 1000-pound cow." He looked away, "but we could build a little memorial for her? On the tree line?" It came out more like a question, rather than a statement.

"I think Annabelle would like that."

"Sure, we can totally do that." He looked over her shoulder, and when Abby peeked back, she caught a glimpse of Diego hurrying around the corner, presumably to figure out how to make a memorial for a cow. She knew they thought she was crazy, but if Betsy was remembered, that's all she cared about.

"Okay, but I still don't know how to ride a horse." Abby's nerves returned. Lucy was a lot taller when Abby was thinking of getting in the saddle than when she was just brushing her down and giving her new hay.

Cole was a surprisingly good teacher. She was so used to his biting remarks or snarky comments, it threw her off to see another side of him. It was good, but it was still strange to see this man she saw as her opposite being gentle and patient. After explaining everything and getting her up on Lucy, he walked her around the paddock, showing her how to ride.

She wasn't going to jump over fences anytime soon, but she was no longer afraid, she was invigorated. As they made their way back to the house, she knew she had to show him what she'd been working on. She hadn't known what she was doing though. She led him to the living room and told him to wait, while she ran upstairs to her bedroom.

"See?" Abby presented her project to him, holding her breath. She didn't think she'd be nervous. But suddenly she didn't know if he would find it as funny as she did.

"Um, what am I looking at?" He held the fabric in his hands, holding it up and turning it this way and that.

"It's a blanket…sort of."

He smiled, glancing at her and back to his hands.

"Abigail, did you learn how to knit?"

"Well, I'm trying. It's not great." She tried to take it back from him, but he pulled it away from her.

"Oh no, this is amazing. Did you do this because I told you to?" He was still grinning at her. She didn't know if he was laughing at her or with her though.

"Well, I started it to be petty, but now I kind of like it. It *is* relaxing. I figured now things have changed, you would like my first knitting project. It's a little wonky though. It's not good. You don't have to keep it." She bit her lip.

"I love it. You sure you want me to have it?"

"Of course. You're the reason I started it in the first

place. I want you to keep it. I thought it would make you laugh when you look at it."

"I won't laugh, thank you." He was gazing at the blanket, no longer grinning. He looked…content.

"Well, we should get going to town. Figure out the supply run," she said. Cole carefully folded the blanket and laid it over the couch, following her out of the house.

* * *

"So, how's it going at Sundown? Cole is still alive, so you haven't gone off the deep end yet, I see." Gabriela sipped on a lemonade, lounging on a stool at Monroe's. They had decided to stop after going to the feed store.

"Great actually. I mean, not great, but you know." Abby sat next to her, drinking her own lemonade, while Cole helped Zach restock the bar. Abby wasn't sure if he should be helping, but he needed something, so he'd stop complaining.

"I have no idea what that means," her friend replied.

Abby sighed. This whole thing with her and Cole was so new she didn't know if she wanted to jinx it by talking about it. Especially with Cole's best friend's wife. But Gabriela was her friend too, and she had no one else to confide in.

"Well, Betsy died. There was some sort of attack.

Annabelle is okay, but well, Betsy didn't make it." Abby's eyes welled up with tears again.

"Oh, sweetie. I'm so sorry." Gabriela pulled her in for a hug, holding on until Abby got her emotions under control.

"Thanks. It's been a hard couple of days."

"But you said it was also great. What's been great about it?"

"Oh, well…" Abby blushed. How did she describe the change between her and Cole?

Gabriela gasped, "you and Cole had sex didn't you!"

"Holy hell, no! We did not. But there may have been a little kissing. And by a little, I mean a very heavy make out session in the hallway. And he wasn't wearing a shirt." She ducked her head, trying to hide behind her hair.

"Well, well, well. Didn't see that coming," Gabriela's voice rang with sarcasm, "so, you aren't going to see Dan anymore? No hard feelings there?"

"Nope. It was a little awkward when he came for a house call to check on Cole though. Cole wanted to know what was going on between Dan and I, but I was so embarrassed. He tried to walk away, we yelled at each other, and BAM, making out. But we're on the same page now I think."

Cole came through the back hallway, catching her eye and grinning. As she smiled back, her heart filled with glee, butterflies erupting in her stomach. That was what she had been missing with Perfect Doctor Dan. Great, now she had picked up Cole's nickname for him.

"Goodness, get a room you two. I don't think we have enough insurance on this place if you burn it down with your smoldering," Gabriela's voice cut off their ogling of one another.

Abby smacked her friend, blushing again. They still needed to talk about where this was going. Abby didn't want to get caught up in something he wasn't on board for, but for now, she wanted to enjoy the newness of it all.

"So, does this mean you're staying?"

"I don't know. I mean, I love it here. I never felt like I belonged in the city, but Sun Oak feels like home. But I don't know if Cole will want me to stay. It's all so new. It feels like everything has changed, but things kind of did a sharp 180. I don't know where his head is at."

"Why don't you ask him? The worst he's going to say is he doesn't know yet, because it's new to him too." Gabriela stole a glance at the two men laughing across the bar. "I've never seen him smile this much though. He wasn't exactly unhappy before, but you knocked something loose in him-woke him up. And I don't want you to leave. It's been hard to find close friends here. I only moved to Sun Oak a couple of years ago, and everyone is small-town nice, but finding women to connect with is hard."

"I know what you mean. I spent five years in the city and Muriel was my only friend. I talked to the people I worked with, but it never went very deep."

Abby hadn't noticed how lonely her life was until she came here. Finding friends when she was an adult was a lot harder than when she was in college. Everyone was experiencing the same thing, but then lives took such different paths and it was harder to connect. When everyone around her got married and started families, it made it even worse.

"Everyone here grew up together. They have such history, breaking into their circle was a battle I couldn't hope to win. But now you're here, and I feel like I have an ally." Gabriela drained her glass and waved it towards Zach for a refill.

"Me too. I *do* want to stay, but if I don't continue working on the ranch, I have no idea what I'd do."

"Why would you stop working at the ranch? I thought Cole said you were making progress."

"He did?"

Gabriela laughed, "yes, silly. He's been saying that for weeks. Once he pulled his head out of his culo and saw how hard you work, he said how nice it was to have someone take over when he had a concussion. Zach tried once when Cole got the flu. I think he is still trying to use up the salt blocks

Zach bought for the goats. And that was two years ago."

"Somehow, we had 17 bags of chicken feed on order this week. I thought I was going crazy! I'm pretty sure Cole ordered it when he was out of it." Abby looked towards Cole, smiling to herself. She had no idea he had noticed how much she had put into the ranch.

"You didn't have to buy that much, did you?! It would take weeks to go through that!"

"No, Adam was able to get others to buy it, but we a good laugh about it."

"I think if you asked Cole, he'd agree you should stick around. You don't want to go back to the city. You don't want to go back to that boring, dead-end job. What would you even do if you didn't stay?"

Abby looked down at her empty glass, contemplating, "I have no idea."

Chapter Twenty-One

Cole

THE days bled together, the hot summer sun beat down on the ranch and extended the daylight long into the evening. Cole started asking the others to finish the evening chores. He used to do it himself since he had nothing else to fill his nights. That changed when his relationship with Abigail had.

Cole couldn't figure out how he had missed so much about her before. His walls had been so thick, he missed how much she made him laugh, how kind she was to others, how encouraging she was to the younger hands. She crashed into his life, breaking down the walls, and forcing him to notice not only her, but the world around him.

Tonight, he was going to put into motion the plan he envisioned the night of the bar fight. He didn't like to think about her other date, but Cole had to admit, he never would have concocted this idea had it not been for Perfect Doctor Dan. Cole wanted to do this earlier, but Abby needed to learn how to ride before he could. And with losing Betsy and dealing with Annabelle, it hadn't felt like the right time.

He was waiting on the porch for her. It was a little strange to try to take someone on a date when you technically lived with them, but he was going to do this right. He wiped his hands down the front of his jeans, careful not to crush the flowers he had for her. He couldn't remember the last time he bought someone flowers.

The door opened and his mouth dropped. She'd worn the blue sun dress that showed off her curves. He'd seen her in a dress before, but somehow this was different. Maybe it was her silky hair, flowing down her back, blowing gently in the breeze, or the happiness radiating from her eyes. No, it was the glowing smile on her face.

"Honey, you look gorgeous," he said when he found his voice, "but you need to change." Abigail's face fell.

Shit.

He didn't want her to think he didn't think she looked amazing, but she couldn't ride in a dress, at least not for long, and not when she just started getting the hang of things. Plus, if he stared at her in that dress any longer, he was liable to pull her back inside, and they'd never make it on the date.

"You look amazing, but we're riding. I want you to be comfortable."

"We're riding?" She looked for the horses, but they were out back though, he wanted to surprise her, but he hadn't thought she'd dress up for him.

"Yup, so get that sexy ass back inside and put on something else. You'll look good in whatever you throw on."

She bit her lip before slipping back through the door. He wasn't going to make it if she didn't get back inside quick. A few minutes later she came out again, in light jeans and a blouse he'd never seen her in before. He was glad he'd worn a nice shirt instead of one of his flannels.

"Still gorgeous," he smiled, handing her the flowers. "Let's get going. We're on a bit of a schedule."

"Okay, let me put these in water."

When she came out again, he led her around the porch to where Lucy and Trigger were waiting. Cole helped her up and they were off. They talked about the ranch as they rode. He tried to steer the conversation to other things, but Abigail kept bringing it back around. Not that he was an expert in romantic conversation, but talking about cattle and goats with other women usually had their eyes glazing over. Abigail's eyes were alight though, as she kept asking questions. She was as immersed in this place as he was.

Topping over the next rise, he slowed to a stop, Lucy

following Trigger's lead. This was his favorite place on the whole property. The fields seemed to roll on forever. A fence ran along the field, stopping the cattle from trampling the picnic Cole asked Brayden to set up before they arrived. He didn't even have to bribe him; it was obvious the boy was smitten with Abigail.

"Oh Cole, this is amazing." Abigail wasn't looking at the picnic though. Her eyes were firmly fixed on the horizon.

"Yeah, it is," he replied, but his own eyes were on her, "come on, let's eat before it gets cold." He dismounted and helped her down, leading her to the blanket spread on the ground. Before she could sit, a moo interrupted them.

"Oh, it's Annabelle! I didn't know you moved her!" Her face lit up, and she hurried towards the fence where the calf was waiting for her.

"We brought her here yesterday. We're still bottle feeding her, but she's big enough to be out here now. It's a good thing you got her to eat, everyone has been taking turns coming out here to give her meals. I think they're as smitten as you are with her." He smiled. He hadn't wanted to tell her the news yet but now was as good of a time as any.

"I'm so glad she's okay. I was worried the others wouldn't be nice to her." She was petting Annabelle's head like she was a puppy instead of a 200-pound cow. And the calf was eating up the attention.

"I've been thinking about what to do with her." He came up and rested his arms on the fence beside them.

"Oh." Abigail's soft reply made his heart ache. "Are you still going to sell her? I'll buy her. I don't know how much it costs, but I'll do it." She wasn't looking at Cole, but he could see the sadness on her face.

"We're going to keep her. She's yours."

She swung towards him, shock and then hope, written on her face.

"Really?! Oh, Cole!" She launched herself so vigorously into his arms he almost didn't catch her, but he laughed. He knew she would be happy, but he hadn't anticipated how pleased her reaction would make him.

"I'm glad you're happy. I'd do it again just to see that smile on your face, Honey." He smiled down at her, hoping she could see what she did to his heart.

"Thank you." She cupped his face, pulling him down to her. Her kiss was sweet, gentle, and the best thanks he could have hoped for. Leaning back, he pulled her to the blanket.

"As much as I'd like to keep kissing you all night, we need to start eating before it goes bad."

As they ate, he asked her about college, her childhood, anything he could think of. He wanted to know everything. He felt like he was making up for lost time, for what he'd missed being blinded by his own insecurities.

Abigail regaled him with some of her more disastrous dating mishaps. She told him about living next to Muriel, and what college was like. She glossed over her parents' death, but he knew this wasn't the time to go into the heavy things. Instead, she launched into some wilder childhood antics she'd gotten up to. She rarely talked about her job though, or her time in the city. He knew she worked with computers or something, but every time he brought it up, she evaded the questions. He didn't want to push it, as the night was going so well.

They watched the sun set, the remnants of their dinner pushed to the side. This is what he had been missing. The peace. Until it washed over him, he hadn't recognized the hole in him, begging to be filled up. Abigail was doing that. He could close his eyes and see the future, for once. Before it had only been Sundown and how he could keep going, keep maintaining. Sitting here with Abigail, he could feel the change. It was slow, gradual, but it was there. That seed of hope, planted by Muriel, was growing because of the woman next to him. He tried to hold back, not rush into anything, but after living so long with blinders on, to see everything so clearly, it was hard to hold back. It was hard not to fall for her. She made it easy. Abigail was someone he never stood a chance resisting, and he was glad he stopped trying.

When there was only a sliver of sun left, he turned, intent

to end this date flawlessly; how he had envisioned all those weeks ago. He glanced around before he went for it.

"What are you looking for?" Abigail asked, following his gaze curiously.

"Just making sure the goats didn't get out," he answered.

"Why would the goats be out this far? They never go further than the house or the horse barn."

"Just making sure. I don't want them ruining this."

"Ruining what?"

Cole leaned in to kiss her, so intent on her lips he didn't register the movement from the corner of his eye.

Mooooo

He'd forgotten to take Annabelle into account. His laughter joined Abigail's as she went to hug the animal, leaving him to follow. He could get used to the joy, in this moment, being with Abigail.

* * *

"Abigail! If you're not down here in ten seconds I'm coming up after you! I'm going to throw you over my shoulder and haul you to the truck." Cole was pacing from the kitchen to the living room. He checked the clock, they were late.

We're going to be even later if I have to go up and get her.

"Hold your horses, Boss. It's your fault I had to go back

and change," she responded, making her way down the stairs.

"My fault? How in the world is it my fault? You're the one who attacked me." He couldn't hide his cocky grin though. It was totally his fault she had to fix her hair again.

"And you're the one who pushed me down on the sofa to continue the 'attack' as you put it." She used air quotes along with an eye roll to emphasize her point. He couldn't help it; she looked delicious and wild when she'd come down the first time.

"I'd do it again if we weren't so late," he said smugly, pulling her in and nuzzling her neck.

Abigail laughed as she pushed him away and linked their arms, leading him through the front door and out to his truck. The last couple of weeks had been a dream. They had fallen into a routine, getting up early and doing chores. He wanted to make up for how hard he tried to keep her out of the ranch by showing her how he ran things. Once night fell, they would make dinner, conversation coming easy. They'd sink on to the couch, her knitting and him reading before they would drop their things to the floor, and he'd pull her on top of him to crash his lips on to hers. He always left her at her door though. Cole wanted her to know he was in this- wholly committed to seeing if they could last.

Sun Oak was alive with people and lights when they made it into town for the annual festival. In past years Cole would stop in and see whatever cattle Diego had chosen to put in the show, but he never stayed. This year though, he wanted to show Abigail everything, starting with which cow he'd picked to compete. He led her to the cattle barn built off of the feed store.

"What's going on here?" Abigail's eyes were wide with wonder as she took in the life teeming around her. There were only about 1,000 people in Sun Oak, but the whole town had come out tonight.

"The cattle show. They do a different contest every year. Last year was "biggest horns". Don't think they'll be doing that again. One of the judges almost got gored by a bull," he cackled at the horror on her face.

"What is it this year?"

"You'll see."

He led her through the barn, sliding around others who called out. For every one person who said hi to him, two others greeted Abigail. Muriel's will may have brought her here, but the townsfolk genuinely liked her. Everyone was enamored with his girl.

"There's Annabelle! Is she in the contest?" Brayden was brushing down the calf's coat, making it shine. "Prettiest Cow? Is that a thing?"

"It is in Sun Oak. They used to show cows professionally, but there wasn't much interest in it the last ten years or so, but they still wanted to keep livestock part of the festival, so they started doing a contest. Everyone votes this year for what the theme should be the following year. This year is 'Prettiest Cow'. Annabelle is going to take the blue ribbon for sure." His eyes twinkled.

"Of course, you will, won't you baby?" Abigail leaned over the fence to stroke Annabelle's side, who gurgled back at her.

"Never heard that noise before, Mr. Cole. Is she okay?" Brayden eyed the calf as if she might explode. He had come a long way being more comfortable on the ranch, but he had a lot to learn.

"Nah, she's fine. Just her happy sound Brayden," Cole told him. He'd never heard a cow make that sound before these two got together, but Annabelle did it every time she saw Abigail these days.

They left Brayden to find food. There were a couple of carnival rides for the kids, but the leading attraction was the games set up by each of the businesses around town. Cole bought a fistful of tickets, wanting Abigail to try every game, but she made him do them with her. She even convinced him to bob for apples. He'd do anything to see her face light up like it was. They went to the beer tent Zach and Gabriela were running with a band playing in the tent.

"They're in high school, think they're going to be the next

big thing. They suckered Zach into letting them do a "set" if you can call the same four songs played over and over again a set," Cole told her. They were terrible, but a lot of people were dancing, cheering them on. Cole was sure most of them were the boys' moms and whoever else they could rope into coming by.

"This is what I love about this place," Abigail said as they walked through another tent, perusing all the pies vying for the blue ribbon.

"What's that?"

"Everyone comes together. The band was terrible, but everyone was supporting them. The little girl back there made her own pie and I'm pretty sure she used salt instead of sugar, but no one was telling her not to enter it, they were telling her how great it was she tried. When you had your concussion people were calling Diego and me, asking if we needed any help around the ranch." She tried a sample of blueberry pie, smiling at the beaming older woman.

"People called to ask if they could help?" Cole hadn't known that. Sure, he'd grown up here and knew everyone in town, but since he'd taken over Sundown, he'd withdrawn more and more every year. He tried to be polite, help when he could, but never would have thought they would call to see what they could do for him.

"Tons of people. Half of the meals came from the diner.

Mrs. Swenson would send meals with Brayden when he showed up in the morning a lot. And Adam sent his kid, Jake to help fix one of the fences that border their property, since it was a long way from the house. Oh! There were also the flowers from Mary, the one who owns the General Store, not the one who sells eggs from her back door." She moved along, sampling two more pies before looking at him.

"What?" she asked.

"I don't think those things were because of me, Honey. I think they did them for you." This was what Muriel had been talking about, a soul who beat for not only Sundown but Sun Oak too. Abigail's soul shined brighter here.

"Oh no, Cole. They did it for you! You grew up here. Why would they do those things for me? I've only been here a couple months. Plus, I wasn't the one hurt, you were."

She couldn't see it. She didn't notice how much she came alive here, as much, if not more than she had woken him up. This was not the timid woman who barely spoke at Harold's office, nor was she the spitfire who yelled at him about goats. Abigail had opened slowly, like the first flower seeing the sun in the spring. Hope bloomed in his chest that maybe he found someone who needed this place as much as he did.

"Even if it was for me, it's only because I got hurt helping you. I don't know if you noticed, but you're a part of this town now. I hope you can see how much you belong here, Abigail.”

He wanted to tell her she belonged here, with him, but he didn't know. What if she still decided to leave? It was already the end of August after all. Cole knew they needed to talk about it, and soon, but the thought of taking that leap, putting himself out there, was too much right now. He wanted to live in these happy moments a little longer, in case she had other plans for her life after the terms of the will were up. He was trying to open up, but he couldn't give her everything until he knew she wouldn't abandon the town, the ranch, and-in the end-him, come October.

ABBY stared at the blue ribbon hanging off the corner of her mirror above her dresser. Almost four weeks earlier, Annabelle had won it at the town festival. These last couple of weeks had been exactly what she wanted when she read Muriel's letter. It was more than she hoped for when she thought about Cole. He was still grouchy in the mornings but gone was the growly asshole she had come to expect. It was like she was seeing him for who he was, rather than who he was hiding behind.

Something was bothering him though. Abby couldn't figure out what it was, and she didn't want to burst the bubble they found themselves in. She caught glimpses of worry in his eyes when he thought she wasn't looking. She would find him on the porch, staring off towards the fields, but when she asked what he was thinking about he would brush her off and kiss her, making her forget she had asked until hours later when she crawled into bed.

Abby sighed. She set the letter she had received on the dresser, picking up her brush instead and swiping it roughly through her hair. Something was off with her too. The letter had pushed her worries back to the forefront of her mind. It was from her boss in the city. She told Gabriela she quit, but that wasn't entirely true. She took a leave of absence and her time was almost up. Abby didn't want to go back. Data entry was boring, managing it wasn't much better. She only took the job, thinking it would be temporary, until she got her feet under her, and paid off her student loans. Those loans had been gone for three years, but she never felt like she her feet were on solid ground. It wasn't until she came here, that she felt like she was healing from her parents' deaths.

Abby was waiting. She knew she should decide on her own, but she wanted to know how Cole felt about her staying. If she moved out of the ranch, did he want her to stay in Sun Oak? He hadn't said, and she was too scared to ask. She knew she needed to and soon. If he wouldn't bring it up, she'd have to. But not today. She'd call her old boss soon and tell him she wasn't coming back, but not today. Today there was too much to do. But on the off-chance things didn't work between Cole and her, she should start looking into other places to live, because she couldn't go back to the city, but she wouldn't be able to stay here either, but not today. Maybe not tomorrow. She'd live in this lovely bubble a bit longer before she brought up the possibility of her staying, and hoped Cole wanted to keep her around.

"Abigail?" Cole's voice floated up from downstairs. He'd been gone the last four days, and while she had been busier than ever, she missed him.

Abby ran, catapulting herself off the last step into his arms, raining kisses on his face. She only now let herself admit how much she ached with him gone.

"Well, I'll leave more often if I get this kind of homecoming," he said, chuckling while he held her.

"Don't you dare. I never want to be left in charge of this ranch again."

She was joking, but his face sobered as he set her back on her feet turned away, and grabbed his bags, suddenly avoiding eye contact. He couldn't think she was serious. He knew how much she loved this ranch, didn't he?

"That bad huh?" He started past her, climbing the stairs.

"No, I was joking. I mean, it's a lot of work, but it was fine. I don't know how you did it by yourself for so long though." She wanted to rewind the minutes, take back what she said, even if she didn't understand what he was so upset him.

"Didn't have a choice, Abigail. I was the only one who stuck around." He opened his door, dropping his bags inside. "I'm going to take a shower." He still wasn't looking at her.

"Hey." She tried to stop him with a hand on his arm, but he kept walking. "Cole. Stop." He didn't.

"Cole Matthew Pierson, stop, and talk to me." She stuck her hands on her hips, trying to make herself as tall as possible.

"That's not my middle name," he said, a dumbstruck expression plastered on his face.

"Well, I don't know your middle name, but I figured it had to be something like Matthew or James or something."

"It's Harlan. After my great-uncle, Muriel's husband." He started to turn back around.

"Hey! I wasn't done yet, Cole Harlan Pierson! You're not going to sulk over this. I don't even know what *this* is." Abby couldn't believe they had to have this conversation again. She knew he wouldn't be able to just switch off the habit. If she had to teach him how to stay and talk, she would.

"I'm tired from the drive. I want to take a shower."

"Bullshit."

"Excuse me?"

"You heard me, I said bullshit. You're not tired. I mean, you might be, but that's not why you're suddenly not able to look me in the eye and why you're walking away."

"I'm looking you right in the eye, Abigail."

"You took offense to what I said downstairs about not wanting to deal with the ranch," she went on as if he hadn't spoken, "I was joking, but you missed that. I said it because I missed you when you were gone. And now you're going to tell me why you reacted like you did."

"Oh, I am, am I?" Cole crooked one eyebrow at her. She'd drag it out of him if she had to.

"Yes, you are. And we'll talk it out if we need to, and then we'll make out...I mean make up." Dammit, she was trying to be stern, but that little slip made his eyes darken and a smirk played on his lips.

"Do we get to make up by making out? Is that what you're saying, Honey?" At least he was back to bantering with her instead of being surly.

"Depends on if you tell me the truth."

"It's hard for me to think someone else loves this place like I do." She waited for him to go on, but he stayed silent.

"And?"

"And what?" He wasn't going to help her here.

"So, when I said I never wanted to be left in charge, you took it to mean I didn't love this place as much as you?"

"I guess so." His eyes were fixed on the ceiling like he didn't want to see a truth he thought he'd find in hers.

"Well, you're right."

"Huh?" His eyes found hers, an incredulous look on his face.

"You're right. I don't love this place as much as you. I can't."

"Why the hell not?"

"Because you built this place, Cole. You've been here your entire life. You put your blood, sweat, and tears into this ranch. You sacrificed to keep it running when no one else would. I haven't. I love Sundown for other reasons, for good reasons, but I can't love it like you do. No one can."

Cole sighed, eyeing her. She wanted to say more, to tell him she was committed, but he didn't give her a chance. He took her face in his hands, cradling it, and rested his forehead against hers.

"Thank you."

"For what?" She asked, resting her hands on his chest.

"For telling me what I needed to hear." He said and kissed her forehead.

"So next time you'll ask instead of walking away, assuming you know what I'm saying?" she murmured into his chest.

"I'll keep trying Abigail. Until I get it right," he answered, folding her into his arms.

They stood like that for a long time, while Abby soaked

up the feeling of relief.

* * *

The days slipped into weeks and before Abby took notice it was halfway through October. The summer sun was fading away, the nights growing more manageable. It didn't ever get that cold, but the rainy season was coming and Cole worked more hours, to make sure the cattle were in the right pastures, and looked up future forecasts to make sure he could rotate them. She learned a lot lately about selling the cattle. She mentioned she wanted to go with him when he went to the auctions in December, but he hemmed and hawed about it before changing the subject.

Abby still hadn't told her boss she wasn't coming back. She didn't know why. At first, she had put it off because it was busy around the ranch, but with the way Cole was acting, she didn't know what to do. It was hard to let go of a sure thing if he still wanted her to leave in a couple of weeks. She tried to bring it up, but every time something interrupted them. She hadn't pushed because she didn't want to stress him out more. That was the excuse she used, but Abby was putting it off, because the final leap felt like stepping into a deep, dark, chasm.

Gabriela brought it up too, each time asking her what she

planned to do, but she kept putting her off. She started searching other ranches in the state, hoping she could find a place that would foster what she'd found at Sundown, but no other ranch came close to what she had here. She knew why though, and it was the people. It was Cole.

"Hey Honey, what are you working on?" Cole's voice jolted her out of her musings. She quickly closed her laptop and turned in the dining chair towards the foyer.

"Oh, nothing. Messing around. The internet is spotty again so everything is loading super slow." She felt guilty, although she hadn't been doing anything wrong. Abby needed to force this conversation soon because she couldn't keep going like this.

"Yeah, it's never been that good this far out of town. You got some time? I want to show you something," Cole asked distractedly.

"Sure, let me grab my purse." She got up, starting for the stairs.

"You won't need it; we're not leaving the ranch."

Abby swung around and slipped on her boots, following Cole as he led her to his truck.

"I thought we weren't leaving the ranch?" she asked as she climbed inside the cab.

"We're not, but it's easier to take the truck out this way."

He pulled it around, back towards the chicken coop, and

drove off down the bumpy path that led through the woods. A couple minutes later the trees gave way and a small cottage came into view. Behind it a creek flowed lazily. It was beautiful, if not a little rundown. It was one-story, small, with a little porch on the front framing a deep green door. The white paint on the shutters was peeling, but the logs were weathered, not rotten. A chimney stuck out from the roof that needed to be repaired.

"Was this Muriel's cottage?" Abby asked as she got out of the truck, mesmerized. It felt like stepping back into time. Like they were in a different world.

"No, this was Uncle Harlan's granddads. He built it when he bought the land. When Harlan married Muriel, the town got together and helped them build the main house."

"It's so peaceful. Is it safe to go in?" She needed to see if the inside was as magical as the outside.

"Sure is. This is where I was staying when I was avoiding you." Cole ducked his head, pulling her up the stairs and opening the door.

"Oh, so you're admitting you were avoiding me?" she teased but stopped short when they crossed the threshold. Its interior was a mix of the old world and new.

The kitchen was upgraded, but the fridge still looked like it was from the 80s. There was a small dining table tucked under the front window in the kitchen. On the opposite side was the living room packed with bookshelves and a couch, flanked by an old recliner. Pictures of the ranch hung on the wall, reminding Abby of Muriel's house in the city. In the corner sat a wood stove that must heat the space, since she saw the walls were made of the same logs as the outside. Cole waited patiently for her to stop gawking, but she couldn't help it.

"Down the hallway that way," he gestured towards the back, "is the only bedroom and a small bathroom. My Dad and I upgraded it when I was a teenager so there would be running water in here. He thought I might want to use this place to get away from everyone else. I don't get to use it as much as I want, but I try to keep it up."

"You don't talk about your dad much." Abby didn't want to pry, but she wanted to hear about his parents.

"Yeah, well, it's not exactly a fun topic to talk about." He took two steps into the living room and sat on the couch, patting the cushion beside him.

She settled in, curling up next to him, saying, "we don't have to if you don't want to."

"No, you should know. Dad died when I was 17. Heart attack. It was sudden. My Uncle Joe, Dad's brother, stayed on a few more years but as soon as Muriel moved to the city, he decided to move on. Think he's in Florida now."

"You don't know?"

Cole was tracing circles on her side, making her shiver, and he tucked her closer to him.

"Not really. He said he didn't want to know anything about the ranch once he was gone. I don't have much else to talk about, so we never kept in touch."

"Why didn't he want to know about the ranch. I thought he grew up here too?"

"He did, but he never wanted to be here forever. He talked about how stifling it was. He always wanted to travel, see the world, but everyone drilled it into his head he needed to stay here, kept the family business alive. Dad was okay with that for the most part. He wanted to leave at one point, but Uncle Joe couldn't stop seeing all the things he was missing."

"Your dad wanted to leave too?" It was like everyone tried to leave when all she wanted to do was stay.

Cole sighed into her hair, pulling her a little closer.

"When I was about ten, he talked about leaving. Muriel and Dad got in a fight about it. I remember them yelling at each other. I snuck out of my room and sat at the top of the steps, listening to Muriel say he was needed on the ranch and Dad was talking about how he shouldn't have to choose between family. I didn't understand much of it at the time, but about two weeks later, Mama left. She tucked me in one night and the next morning she was gone. I thought she'd gone on a trip. That wasn't something I'd remembered her doing before, but I was convinced that's all it was. She never came back."

"You haven't seen her since?" she asked, once she was certain her voice wouldn't waver.

"I haven't seen her, talked to her, don't know where she is. If Dad ever knew, he never said. I asked him why she left when I was older, and he said, 'sometimes it's not in the soul to stay'. I didn't know what he meant, but Muriel wrote something like it in her letter. Dad's explanation makes a lot more sense now."

Abby wanted to ask what Muriel had written to him, but she wasn't ready to share her own letter, so she couldn't ask Cole.

"So, you took over at 19? I mean, couldn't have been easy, but growing up on the ranch must have helped, right?"

"You'd think, but no," Cole admitted, "The old foreman was a guy who had been with us for years. He got it in his head Muriel would let him take over instead. He wasn't very happy to have to suddenly take orders from a kid. When he left, he took half the workers with him. The ones who stayed either took off after a year or quit ranching altogether."

"How did you run things? Tell me you didn't do it all yourself." She didn't think it was possible, to run an entire cattle ranch all alone, but Cole was laughing again.

"I think I would have died by the third day if I tried to do it myself. No, I called up every kid around my age, told them I'd pay them double until I had a full crew, and then either give them a severance to move on or hire them on in senior positions if they'd drop everything to come help me. I hired Diego the same way. About a year after I took over, I was still struggling to find someone to be the foreman and Diego was 18, coming through town looking for work. I told him I'd hire him, same deal as the rest of the guys I'd taken on the year before. He ended up being the best one I took a chance on. I made him the foreman when he was 20. Everyone thought I was crazy, but I had a feeling about him. Couple years later Gabriela came to visit and neither of them left."

"I can't imagine. I mean, I sort of ran things when you were hurt, and then when you went to the auction, but it was overwhelming. To have to do it all the time at that age? I would have laid down in the goat pen and let them nibble me to death," Abby shuddered.

"Aw, Honey, I'm sure you would have done fine. Sometimes you do what needs getting done and you think of how hard it was later."

Cole's words jarred something in her brain. She needed to let go of her life in the city and stop thinking of how hard things were until later. After she told her boss she was quitting, she'd talk to Cole about the future. At this moment she needed to stop holding on to safe and do it for real. She knew she would never go back, now it was time to actually do it.

"I think that's what I did after my parents died."

Cole hugged her tighter, waiting. She talked about them with Muriel, but she hadn't gone into too much detail. She felt like she needed to with him though.

"I had just turned 22, senior year of college. I was trying to finish my psychology degree, but I had two years left. A police officer showed up at my door at 3 a.m. My roommates had been drinking, not anything wild, but they thought the police were there for them. They weren't. A deer ran out in front of their car. Dad tried to swerve and ended up hitting a tree. They both died at the scene."

"Abigail, I'm so sorry." He kissed her head again, squeezing her to him.

"It's okay. It's easier to talk about now. My friends didn't know how to handle it. None of them had lost a parent, much less both of them at the same time. Suddenly, I had to make all these plans and deal with their estate. I didn't even know what an estate was before that. So, I switched my major to business, graduated early, sold my childhood home, and took the first job I could get out of state. I bought my house with the money my parents left me and Muriel was sitting on her porch when I started moving in. She bullied me into having a cup of tea right then and there, even though I hated tea."

"Wait, you hate tea?" Cole leaned back, a look of shock on his face.

"Not anymore. She made me learn to love it. She also helped me not fall into depression. I was living for a routine at that point. I didn't have any friends; I was running away from the memories of my parents. She made me open up and talk, and she showed me that even though my routine allowed me to survive, I needed to learn how to live again."

"She was always good at that. After mom left, she helped raise me. Dad was off in his own head for a while, trying to lose himself in the ranch. Guess I followed in his footsteps more than I realized."

Cole stretched as he stood up, "enough heavy talk. I'll make some dinner and you can go explore. Be careful if you go outside, with the recent rains, the bank on the creek gets a little soft."

It didn't take Abby long to investigate the rest of the cottage, but outside she took her time. The birds were calling to each other and the cicadas were buzzing, almost drowning out the water of the creek flowing by. Cole called to her after a while, and she made her way back.

They ate and talked about other things, both of them quieter after revealing so much to the other. Abby couldn't help but admire how much Cole had overcome and how strong he had been to keep the ranch thriving. She understood a little more now why this place was so special to him. It wasn't just his legacy; it was in his soul.

"You okay staying here tonight?" he asked as she perused the bookshelves stuffed with old farmer's almanacs and historical romances.

She peeked over her shoulder and gave him a suggestive look, "I don't have my pajamas."

"Not a problem Abigail."

"You know there's only one bed, right?" she raised an eyebrow at him, a smile pulled at her lips.

Cole's eyes darkened as he prowled closer, "we'll only need one bed tonight, Honey."

Chapter Twenty-Two
Cole

THE past week had been a dream. Waking up each morning with Abigail was better than he had imagined. The best part of Cole's day was waking up with her in his arms. He pulled her closer, and she sighed in her sleep, relaxing more into him. He could feel the pull of his heart, telling him to take the final leap. Today was it.

It was a Sunday, one week before the will expired, and Cole was going to ask her to stay. He couldn't imagine her saying no, since she was so happy, but nerves tingled along his spine as he thought about it. It seemed like such an easy question to ask, but in reality, he felt like he was asking for more than time. He would be asking her to accept all that came with this life-to accept him. He slipped out of bed, leaving her to sleep while he made breakfast. As he was about to bring it up to her though, she glided down the stairs, deliciously rumpled in her pajamas, messy hair thrown in a bun.

"Good morning, Honey. I was going to bring you breakfast in bed."

She yawned and mumbled, "you want me to go back up?" She could barely keep her eyes open.

"You look exhausted. You should go back to bed."

"You're the one who kept me up half the night."

Her tired smile was a balm to his soul. How could she refuse to stay with him? She was content, beyond a doubt. Cole came around the island, leaning down to hug her from behind as she sat. He kissed her head, breathing in her scent, not wanting to let go of this moment yet. He started to say something, but his phone pinged with an alert. He picked it up and grumbled

"Shit, I have to make the deposit for the auction. I'll be right back."

Abigail nodded sleepily after him, sipping the tea he handed her. He smiled, watching her for a moment drinking out of her ridiculous mug he learned Muriel gifted her. Apparently, Muriel never served her tea in anything else. He huffed out a laugh, remembering how he wanted to smash it when she first moved in. Cole made his way to his office, searching for his computer, but it was nowhere to be found. They had spent more time at the cottage this past week, but he couldn't remember if he left it there or not.

He went back to the kitchen he asked, "have you seen my computer? I have to make this payment but I can't do it from my phone." He scanned the room, searching.

"I think you left it at the cottage, been there for at least two days." Her head was resting on her arms, and she was almost asleep.

"Can I borrow yours?"

"Uh huh." She yawned again, waving towards the table, where it sat. He didn't think he was going to serve her breakfast anytime soon, much less ask her to stay, at least until she was fully awake.

Opening up her laptop, an envelope was tucked inside. It was addressed to Abigail, but he didn't recognize the return label while he set it aside. The last thing he wanted to do was snoop through her things. He waited while it started, gazing out the window. The goats were out of the pen again, grazing in the front yard. He had half a mind to pound on the window in retribution, but he didn't want Abigail to faint too.

His eyes slid back to the screen and he froze. Right there was an email, addressed to Abigail. He didn't mean to pry, but it was clear what it was with only a cursory scan. It was from her boss in the city, asking how country life was and when she was coming back. Confusion clouded his face as he glanced at Abigail and back to the email. He thought she said she quit her job. Maybe her old boss was trying to get her to come back. The email was dated the day before, but his eyes lit on the envelope sitting harmlessly on the table next to him. The return address matched the signature on the email.

He looked to Abigail again, but she was still resting her head at the breakfast bar. Cole knew he shouldn't, but a worrying thought crossed his mind. Had she quit? Maybe she never planned to stay, even now, after everything they had been through.

Instead of opening it, he picked it up and walked over to the woman he was sure he was falling for.

"What's this?" he asked. He tried to temper his voice, but gruffness rang through.

"Huh?" She lifted her head, dull eyes fighting to focus, but as soon as she spied what he was holding her eyes grew wide.

"What's this, Abigail?" There had to be an explanation. She would tell him he was being crazy, that there was nothing to worry about, he would ask her to stay, and they'd continue, slowly but surely, building a life together.

"Uh, well, it's just a letter from my job in the city."

"The job you quit right?"

"Umm…" Her eyes were fixed on the envelope instead

of him.

"You said you quit when you moved here. You wanted to learn about the ranch. I thought we were on the same page with this."

He hadn't specifically asked her to stay, but he thought he'd made it clear with his actions. Her shoulders slumped, and she stared at the tea in her mug.

"I didn't actually quit."

"What does that mean?"

"I took a leave of absence."

That made sense. Before she had gotten here, hell, even after the first couple of months, she hadn't known she would stay, so of course, she would take a leave of absence instead of outright quitting. He felt his shoulders relax and relief trickled through him.

"Okay, but you told them you weren't coming back now, right?"

"I didn't. I mean, I haven't. Yet. I was going to, but I haven't." Abigail looked at him, tears filling her eyes.

"Why didn't you? I know we haven't talked about it, but it was obvious to me you were going to stay. You told me you didn't like your job or your life in the city."

"I don't know! At first, I didn't know if I would find a place here. After I just didn't bother with it, but then I didn't know where this thing between us was going." Her hands came up to cover her face and then her words sunk in.

Couldn't be bothered? And how could she not know where things were going? Rationally, he knew he worried about the same things, but she had actual ties to sever-houses to sell, jobs to quit, things to pack. She'd been projecting that all she wanted was to keep calling this place home. He had been worried she wouldn't want to stay, even if all the signs said otherwise, which was a rational fear for him. After all, he went through, all he had told her, it was natural for him to be nervous. But while he was certain she would stay, and it was a formality to ask, she had been trying to decide whether it was worth it, whether *he* was worth it to quit her job, pack up her life, and move here permanently.

"And after?" He could hear the last sliver of hope in his question.

"I got panicky!" she cried out; her voice muffled. That sliver floated away with her words.

"Panicky." It wasn't a question. It was a confirmation of all his uncertainties.

"I know. Things were going so great and I didn't know what to do."

Were. They *were* going great, but now she was backing out. Now that she faced the reality of staying in this podunk town, working a ranch day in and day out, she couldn't handle it. Making the final leap was too much, too hard.

"You told me you felt alive here, that Sundown woke you up. You told me you felt hope here, with me. I didn't think it was a crazy concept we were on the same page when it came to the future," his voice was full of accusation.

"It wasn't! It isn't!"

"Liar," he said, dropping the letter next to her.

He had to get away, lose himself in work or the land, anything, before he let her brainwash him again. Her tormented gaze met his. Cole couldn't help but sneer, as his heart broke more. He couldn't let her see how much she hurt him. He pulled the mask of anger on, banishing the pain.

"Well, I hope you liked your vacation from the real world."

"You can't think I saw this as a vacation," she cried, reaching towards him, but he stepped back. If she touched him, he'd crumble. Now that he started, he couldn't stop the hateful words from spewing from his mouth.

"You think you can waltz in here, take half of what's rightfully mine? Just play around for a while, slum it with us hicks, before you go back to the city, with my money in your pocket and a story to tell all your friends. It must have been so easy for you, knowing this wouldn't be your life forever. That you could sample it for a bit and flit away again. Back to your comfortable life, far away from the dirt and the work and all us here."

"Cole, no. I never saw it that way. I wanted to stay. I *want* to stay."

"I don't believe you. All you've done is lie. You lied about quitting your job. What else have you lied about? Did you lie about the will? Did you know all along what Muriel planned to do? Did you manipulate her into this?" Her mouth hung open, no words coming out. "The worst part of this is I believed you. I fell for every single one of your lies. I thought you cared about me and this ranch. But you're just like them." Cole knew he should stop, should walk away, but he couldn't help it. He would do anything, say anything, to stop this pain.

"Like who," she whispered.

"Like everyone who leaves this place behind-starting with my mother. But you're more like Jen because you made me believe you felt something, that you wanted this life. But it wasn't enough for either of you was it, Abby?"

I wasn't enough for either of you.

Cole spun away, holding on to his anger, burrowing it into his heart, hopelessly trying to use it to build back his walls he had carefully constructed all these years.

"Cole!" she called after him as he stalked towards the door, pulling his boots on without bothering with socks. He didn't stop to tie them either. Cole could hear her rushing after him. He had to get away. He snatched his keys off the hook, swung open the door, and slammed it shut behind him. Blocking her off from him and his heart.

* * *

Cole pulled his car into Monroe's. They weren't open on Sundays, but he prayed Zach would be there. As he pounded on the back door, he kept seeing Abigail's face, shell shocked and broken; guilty.

Good.

She deserved to feel guilty. He tried to push her from his mind, but she kept creeping back in. His own words played over in his mind. He didn't know where all it came from. It was like he opened his mouth and all his insecurities fell out. Zach swung the door open, and glared at him. Great, Abigail called Gabriela, who turned around and immediately told Zach. This is why he didn't want them to be friends in the first place.

"Don't start," he spat, pushing past his friend. Coming into the bar area he saw Gabriela grab her purse. She shot him a look of loathing before she started for the door. The lecture from her was coming, but not now at least. Now that the anger was draining from him, he was exhausted. There was a stabbing pain in his chest instead of the white, hot fury that had been there since Abigail's confession.

"If she leaves because of you, I'll never forgive you," she said facing the door before she pushed it open, and disappeared to comfort her friend. Cole sighed. She'd forgive him, they had been friends for years now. She couldn't be mad at him forever.

"She's serious man. I've never seen her so angry at someone, me included, and we both know I did some dumb shit when she first got here."

"Quite a pair, aren't we?" Cole collapsed on to a stool, hanging his head in his hands.

"Except when I pulled my head out of my ass, I didn't go back to being a complete dick. What the hell happened?" Zach poured him some water.

"Thought you knew." Sullenly, he picked up the glass, draining half of it in one go. Didn't numb the pain like whiskey would, but he wasn't about to start drinking this early in the morning.

"I picked up on her version of things through the sobs, but I want to know your side." Zach leaned against the bar.

"She didn't quit her job."

"So?"

"What do you mean 'so'? She said she quit her job and didn't. Still hasn't. She lied."

"Okay, did you ask why?" Zach looked at him, making him feel like an idiot.

"Of course, I asked her. She said she couldn't be bothered, and she didn't think we were going anywhere, and she panicked. Things were going well and then they weren't. She was never on board. I don't know what parts of her story to believe anyways."

"Are you sure that's what she meant?" Zach's skepticism started to piss him off.

"Certainly didn't defend herself." He shook his head, gazing at the bottles lined behind the bar, "I can't believe I fell for it again."

"Ahh." Zach grabbed a rag and started wiping down the bar, though it was spotless.

"What's that supposed to mean?"

"Listen, man, I know it hasn't been easy for you. I was there. I remember what you were like when your mom left. And I was there when Jen left too." He looked like he wanted to say more, but he kept wiping the counter.

"Jen didn't just hurt me. It wasn't like we just broke up."

"No, she tore your heart out-led you to think you would be together forever after she graduated from college. I know it gutted you when you caught her cheating. She was a bitch to say all that shit about you not being enough; about no one ever going to stick around. Again, I was there. But Cole, Abby isn't Jen. And she isn't your mom."

"I know that."

"Do you? Because from what I heard, you told Abby she was exactly like them. I'll have your back no matter what. That's what we do. So, if you honestly don't think you can have a future with her, let her go. Let her find someone that'll love her like she should be loved. But if you think that someone might be you, then pull your head out of your ass and apologize."

"I think that's the same speech I gave you when Gabby was going to take that job overseas," Cole smiled, remembering how shocked Zach looked when he gave that advice.

"It was. It's an excellent speech, and it stuck in my brain. You were right then and it's still true now. I had to figure out if I was worthy of her, if I could give her what she deserved. I knew I loved her. You might not be there yet. But the speech still works. You either have to apologize and work through it or let her go. She deserves that much from you." Zach went back to wiping down the bar, leaving Cole to wonder if he made a mistake; one he would someday need to fix.

Chapter Twenty-Three

Abby

"I don't understand what happened. I mean, one minute he was making breakfast and, the next he was so angry," Abby cried into Gabriela's shoulder.

"It wasn't your fault. He's the one being stupid. That one never thinks before he speaks." Gabriela was rubbing her back gently, but the tears kept coming.

"He's right though. I did lie. I didn't mean to lie, but I didn't quit my job. I didn't know how. He never said he wanted me to stay. I was going to do it, but I was so scared. And if I quit, I'd have nothing. No job, no future, nothing," she sobbed.

"Oh sweetie, that's not how it works." Gabriela pushed her back, forcing Abby to look at her. "You knew you weren't going back, no matter what he decided. You knew you couldn't. You hated that job and the city. Muriel gave you the push, but there was no way you could slip back into your old life. Too much has changed. You changed. But if things don't work out between Cole and you, you'll still have yourself. You'll still have who you've become."

"I know. I mean, I do. I hate how this turned out. I feel like I'm losing more than Cole. I'm losing the ranch too. And the people and the…purpose, I guess. I felt like I had a purpose here. But without all this, I don't know what to do." Despair clawed at her. She knew she would eventually be fine if Cole didn't forgive her, but it was like losing a whole way of life she wanted to keep. Ironic, since the only place she felt like herself was here, and he accused her of not wanting it.

"Then fight for it." Gabriela nodded as if it was easy.

"I don't know how."

"Apologize. Tell him you are sorry for lying, but you love this place and you love him and you want to stay. That this is the place you belong."

"Do I love him?" Abby didn't know herself. She knew she was falling for him, but how did someone know if they were in love? She knew the anguish flooding through her was like nothing she'd felt before. The misery and pain she felt every time she imagined his face, so full of betrayal, overwhelmed her.

"You wouldn't be this upset if you didn't love him, Abigail."

Hearing Gabriela call her Abigail instead of Abby set her off again. It felt strange to hear it from someone else.

"Oh god, Gabriela, he called me Abby." Obviously, Gabriela didn't understand, because she looked at her like Abby has gone off the deep end.

"Does that matter?" she asked cautiously.

"He never calls me Abby! He always calls me Abigail. He's never going to forgive me. Oh my god, what if he starts to hate me? What if I can never fix this?" Abby wailed, falling into her friend's arms. At least she knew she could count on Gabriela because she didn't see how she could ever get Cole to trust her again.

* * *

Abby gave him two days, based on Gabriela's advice. She would give him the time to cool off, get some sense knocked into him by Zach, and she'd apologize and try to explain better. She was worried he wouldn't listen. But none of that would matter if she couldn't find him. He hadn't been back to the house, at least that she had noticed. He must have come back for clothes at some point, but she couldn't bring herself to check his room. Abby avoided going anywhere near the barns. She fed the goats and the chickens each morning. She went to visit Annabelle, who was in the lower field, learning how to wean. She tried to give him the time and space Gabriela told him he needed.

This morning she did her chores and afterward set off for the barn, determined to find Cole. But he wasn't there and Brayden, the only one she could find, hadn't seen him. She went to the horse barn but Trigger was still in his stall, nickering at her. Abby circled back to the house, walking the fence line, shielding her eyes to see if she could spot him, but all she saw was grass and cows.

At the house, she ventured into his room, but nothing looked like it had changed. Abby avoided it since their fight, going back to her own room, crying herself to sleep the first night. She tossed and turned the night before. The mattress felt different and it smelled musty, even though she slept in it less than two weeks ago. An emptiness was seeping into the house the more time passed.

His truck had been at the barn, so he hadn't gone into town unless someone else took him, but that wasn't like him. The cottage. He ran away there once before, of course he'd be there. She hurried off down the path. The walk was long enough for her to get too far into her head, worrying about what-ifs.

The trees parted and revealed the cottage. Every time she came, she felt like it was welcoming her, urging her to come in and stay awhile. Scanning around she didn't see any signs of Cole, but maybe he was inside, or at the river. It was higher than she'd last seen it with the recent rains.

"Abigail. What are you doing here?" Abby looked around, still not seeing him. "Up here." Cole's voice came again. He was on the roof, a tool belt hanging low over his hips, pulling his jeans down, revealing a slice of skin when his white t-shirt rode up.

Forcibly pulling her gaze away from the sight that sent heat thrumming through her. The last thing she needed was to get all hot and bothered when they had fought. There was no anger in his eyes though, it was resignation. At least he was back to calling her Abigail.

"Hi."

That's all you got Abby?

"Did you need something?"

"Can we talk?" She bit her lip, hoping he wouldn't freeze her out again.

"I'm a little busy here."

"It won't take long." At least she hoped it wouldn't.

"Yeah, fine," he sighed and disappeared to the back of the cottage.

"Hi," she said again when he appeared a minute later.

He took off the gloves and slapped them against his palm once.

"What did you want to talk about." He wasn't looking at her, his eyes focusing over her shoulder.

"I wanted to say I'm sorry."

"For what?" With him not meeting her gaze, she felt like she was talking to a wall.

"I should have told you I didn't quit my job. And I should have talked to you about why I didn't. It was hard to let go of my security net. I was worried you wouldn't want me to stay. I tried to bring it up, but not as much as I should have. I should have communicated more, but I didn't want to burst the bubble we were living in."

The last couple of days she thought a lot about what she wanted to say to him. She knew she had to be honest since she had avoided it before. That wasn't fair to him. The last few days shed light on why she had avoided the conversation. It stemmed from him, but she wasn't going to accuse him of anything. Then they'd never get anywhere. When it came down to it, she should have brought it up, regardless of whether she was ready for the answer or not.

"Okay."

Okay? That was it? Did that mean he forgave her? Did he still think she was like Jen? Did he still want her to stay?

"I, uhh, emailed my boss and told him I'm not coming back." Abby wanted him to know how committed she was, but his lack of reaction to her apology made her nervous. He was still pushing her away, freezing her out.

"Sounds good."

"So where does that leave us?"

She needed to know he still wanted her here, that he still wanted her, but he wasn't giving her anything. She couldn't figure out what he was thinking and it terrified her. Cole sighed, looking down and cuffing the gloves on his leg. The silence stretched on. The longer it lasted, the more her heart cracked.

"You should call your boss back; say you changed your mind." He stared at the ground, still not meeting her eyes.

"Why would I do that?"

No, no, no. Don't do this.

"I think it's better this way."

"I don't think it's better this way. You were right. I hated that job. Even if I didn't…well, I still won't go back."

She couldn't bring up staying now he dropped that on her. While she spent the past few days thinking about how to fix this, he had been looking for a way out of it; a way to let her down gently. To make the end official, instead of fighting for them.

"It's for the best."

Abby caught the sob in her throat before it could escape. She didn't want to cry in front of him. She didn't want him to see how shattered her heart was. The dreams that had been forming in her mind winked out, one by one. The more she stood there, trying to get her emotions under control, the more the hurt gave way to anger. At the first sign of trouble, he turned tail and run. Shutting her out and giving up.

"You're a coward," she hissed. She glared at him through the tears she refused to let fall.

"Excuse me?" His head snapped up. Good-he would see how livid she was.

"You heard me. You're a coward. You hide behind your fear of people leaving. You never let anyone get too close because they might do something that will hurt. You build your walls so high; no one could ever breach them. But you don't want them to. Because if you never let anyone in, you'll never get hurt. You were always going to be waiting for something to go wrong, for some obscure reason to pop up so you could seize it and use it against me. To prove that you're right. You would always be waiting for me to leave. You never wanted to fight for this, you were looking for it to fail as soon as we got past all the bullshit. Well, go ahead. Hide behind your walls and be alone forever, because I can't do this anymore. I can't be the only one trying."

Cole stared at her, a blank expression on his face. She waited, hoping he would disagree, that he would tell her she was wrong. She waited for him to yell or scoff or fight-fight for them, for her. But all she was met with was a deafening silence and that blank, expressionless look in his eyes. It was clear he didn't care anymore. Maybe he never had.

Chapter Twenty-Four
Cole

HE was on the roof again. He was trying to replace some shingles on the cottage before the rain started, but he couldn't concentrate on what he was doing. Abigail's words kept ringing in his ears. It was like she had held up a mirror, showed him who he truly was, and they had both found him lacking. She was right. He was a coward.

The purring of a car echoed down the path. Cole's heart pounded, anxiety and longing filling him as he strained to see if Abigail's car would appear. He let out a deep sigh when Zach came around the bend and made its way through the potholes that had grown deeper with the recent storms. It must be important if Zach was willing to risk his precious classic car getting banged up in the mud-filled divots.

"What's up?" he called down when Zach had parked.

"Oh, nothing. Wanted to see if you needed any help." Cole scanned Zach from head to toe, starting with the polo shirt he was wearing down to the sneakers on his feet.

"You thought you would help fix a roof wearing that? Bullshit." He had come to lecture him some more.

"Alright, I'm only here because Gabby told me to come. I told her to leave it alone, you gotta figure things out for yourself, but she insisted. So here I am." He spread his arms wide, smiling.

Cole rolled his eyes and tried to get back to work. He prayed Zach would leave if he ignored him, and he could have some peace and quiet for once.

"Haven't seen Abby around. Have you?" Zach asked innocently.

"Thought we weren't going to talk about it?" He hammered in another nail, securing the shingle.

"I got some time to kill. Might as well make some small talk."

"You can always hang out inside. Or make yourself useful and make some coffee instead."

"Nah, think I'll just watch you avoid your problems for a while."

Smartass.

He worked in silence for the next few minutes, shingle,

nail, hammer, check, repeat. Then it hit him what Zach had said.

"Wait, you haven't seen Abigail?"

"Thought we weren't going to talk about it?" Zach asked him slyly.

"We're not."

Cole grimaced and got back to work. Where had she been though? Cole hadn't been back to the house. He only went to the ranch when he was certain Abigail wasn't going to be around. Instead, he made Diego come to him. The foreman hadn't mentioned her either, but he did throw the occasional knowing look in Cole's direction.

"Gabriela keeps trying to call her, but she doesn't answer. I stopped by and talked to Diego too. He said the morning chores are still getting done, but he hasn't seen her either."

Cole grunted in response. He didn't care and there were only three days left before she was supposed to leave. He'd go to Harold's and see if she had done the paperwork to sign her shares of the ranch to him-mail her a check. He wouldn't have to see her before she walked out of his life forever.

"Thought I saw her car over at Harold's office on Wednesday," Zach threw out in an innocent voice.

Cole still didn't respond. Would she have left already? Did a couple days void Muriel's will?

Zach kept talking, "you think she's trying to take the

ranch?"

"No," Cole snapped back, "Abigail wouldn't do that."

"Thought you were back on her being a con artist. Wouldn't she want to take the whole ranch if she could? Sell it off and get the most bang for her buck?" Zach was baiting him, but he couldn't resist falling into the trap.

"She's not a con artist. Abigail wouldn't try to take Sundown from me. She's too good a person to do something like that."

Zach's eyebrows shot up as Cole glared at him.

"Well, if she's such a wonderful person, and you think so highly of her, why are you here instead of beggin' her to stay?"

"It's for the best."

"The best for who? You?"

"No, the best for her. You were right, she deserves someone worthy of her. I'm not right for her."

"God, you really are an idiot, aren't you? I didn't spout back that speech to you so you could give up. I told you so you would man up and apologize!"

"Doesn't matter. She wants something I can't give her."

"She wants you, dumbass."

"Maybe she did, but she said she's done trying. Couldn't do it anymore. She shouldn't have to keep fighting. It shouldn't be this hard. If I was right for her, it would have been easier."

It was hard for him to admit he wasn't enough for her, but he cared about her and wanted her to be happy. She'd get over it. And so would he…hopefully.

"Is that what you think? That being in a relationship is easy? It's not. It's constant work. It's constantly battling against your fears and theirs. It's fighting for it because the alternative is a bleak wasteland without them. When the devastation of losing her hits, I hope she's willing to take you back you shithead." Zach threw up his hands again and stomped back to his car and peeled away.

Cole didn't know how long he stood on the roof, staring off into the trees where Zach disappeared. He knew his friend was right, but he also knew Zach missed the point. He knew relationships took work, that it wasn't easy. He didn't think it had to be as hard as it had been with Abigail though. Cole knew she deserved someone who could fight for her. Cole just didn't know if he had any fight left in him.

* * *

Friday Cole was forced to go into town. He wanted to send someone else to get the supply order, but Diego said they couldn't spare anyone. There was supposed to be a big storm coming and it was all hands-on deck. Guilt ate away at him, knowing he should be on the ranch more, helping move the cattle to higher ground or into shelters. The lower pasture always flooded this time of year, but they were behind in getting the small herd moved to the shelter.

He scanned the streets for Abigail's car since he hadn't seen it at the house when he pulled out, but he didn't see it in town either. Had she gone back to the city? It wasn't a long drive, but she still had until Sunday, according to the will. Cole didn't care about the shares. Not anymore. But it was easier to focus on the conditions instead of thinking about how empty the house would be when Abigail moved out. He could fix up the cottage some more and move there instead. It wasn't like he needed all the space at the main house, especially with her gone.

Jake, was waiting for him when he pulled up to the feed store. Cole had called and left a message for Adam to have everything ready. The last thing he wanted was to get caught in chitchat with someone from town.

"Hey there Mr. Cole!" Jake smiled but was empty-handed. No pallet, no feed, nothing.

"Hey, Jake. I called your dad, asking him to have my order ready to load. You know if he got it?"

"Oh yeah, he totally got it." Jake stood there; a grin plastered on his face.

"Okay, so where is it?" If this kid didn't start talking, he was going to strangle him.

"Miss Abby picked it up earlier. We kind of wondered why you were coming if she got it, but Dad thought you needed something else, and we missed it. So, he sent me to get whatever else you needed."

Abigail picked it up? In what? Her old car wasn't big enough to haul everything, much less make it back with all the extra weight. It only started every third week during a blue moon anyways. Maybe she borrowed Diego's truck instead.

"What was Abigail driving when she picked it up?"

"Oh, you haven't seen her new truck? It's a beauty, I tell ya. Don't tell her, but I laughed when I spotted her. I could barely see her over the steering wheel," Jake hooted.

"Nope, haven't seen it yet. Guess we must have gotten our signals crossed. I didn't know she was picking the supply order up today. Sorry to make you stand out here."

"No problem Mr. Cole. Kind of nice to have a break. Dad's freaking out about the storm. He's been making me pile sandbags along the back wall of the warehouse, thinks it might flood."

"He thinks it's going to be that bad?"

"Yeah. Mrs. Swenson is closing the diner early tomorrow too. Said it's supposed to hit in the evening and go through the weekend. They're talking a lot of rain, some hail. Dad said if you need extra help at the ranch to let us know."

"I think we're all set, or we will be by the time it starts. Tell him thanks though." Cole waved to Jake as he drove away. He didn't have time to wonder about Abigail's new truck or why she picked up the supply order. The storm was coming before he anticipated, and they weren't ready. He rushed back to the ranch, hoping they'd get everything done before the sky dumped on them.

Chapter Twenty-Five
Abby

ABBY watched the ranch hands rushing back and forth from the back porch. She wanted to help, despite the fact she might see Cole, but Diego sent her back to 'batten down the hatches' on the house. She didn't know what that meant, but she'd done the best she could. Brayden had pulled up with sandbags they stacked along the backside of the porch.

She still hadn't seen Cole, but he was probably out in the fields. Abby knew he wouldn't hide at the cottage with this big of a storm coming, just to avoid her. The ranch was his priority. At this point though, she felt useless. The sky was darkening but there was no rain. It was maddening, like an ax hanging over their heads, with no inkling when it would fall.

Abby turned and went back inside. She still had to pack

up the things she'd been putting off until the last possible minute. She told herself it was because she was busy with the ranch or that it was too daunting a task to do, but she knew better. Abby was waiting for Cole to change his mind. As the hours ticked by though, her hope dwindled little by little. She spent the rest of Saturday alternating between watching the sky and packing up her things. She didn't think she brought that much, but her things had scattered throughout the house without her noticing. That evening, Gabriela pulled up, letting herself in armed with dinner.

"I thought the diner was closing early?" Abby asked as she took the sacks.

"They did, this is greasy bar food. Figured we'd go all out for your last night here." Gabriela frowned at her.

"Don't be like that. I'll come visit." Abby got plates and started pulling things out as her friend settled on a stool.

"Really? You might run into Cole."

"Yes, I will. Not at first, of course, so you'll have to visit me instead."

"I don't understand why you're going back to the city," she rolled her eyes.

"Because I own a house there. And I'll need to find a new job." They'd talked about this before, but Gabriela wouldn't let it go.

"You could find a job here. Zach would hire you."

"Oh yes, that would be lovely," she answered sarcastically, "'Welcome to Monroe's, hello to you too Cole whose best friend is now my boss. What can I get you to drink?' Because that wouldn't be awkward at all."

"He'd have to deal, they both would. You could stay."

"Gab, you know I can't do that," she said somberly. "This is his town, his place in the world. I can't keep intruding on it when I'm not wanted here."

"But I want you here." Gabriela hugged her.

"And that means a lot, but it's not enough. You know that. I can't stick around to have my heart broken every time we cross paths. I'll never move on if I have to see him all the time."

"Do you think you'll be able to move on? I don't know if I would have if Zach and I hadn't worked out our issues. I'd most likely be living overseas, miserable."

"I don't know. My heart hurts too much to know if I'll be able to heal. Right now, I need to focus on one thing at a time. The first step is going back to the city, to maybe sell my house. Something changed in me here, and I need to see if I can find that elsewhere."

"You really think he's not coming? That he won't change his mind?"

"No, not anymore."

* * *

* * *

The rain started at midnight. With how everyone was talking, she thought it would be gale-force winds, and a volley of hail and showers, but instead, it started softly, a slow pattering of rain on her window. She stayed up late into the night, straining her ears to hear Cole come in, but when she finally fell asleep, he still hadn't appeared.

The next morning, she hurried to pack up her new truck between breaks in the rain. She backed it up to the porch, so she could reach into the bed, since she wasn't tall enough to load it with the topper on. She almost told the guy she bought it from she didn't need the topper, but thought better of it. It was a good thing she did as the driveway was a land mine of mud holes already. Once everything was in, she sat at the island, clutching the blanket she had knitted. It was lopsided and some holes were larger than others. Abby didn't know if she should leave it-if Cole would even want it anymore. The memories she built during her short time here played in her head.

She thought she could be happy here. That she found home. Abby didn't want to admit defeat. She wanted to run out and find Cole and make him listen, but she knew it wouldn't make a difference. Every time she got the urge, she remembered the look on his face the last time they talked.

That blank, vacant look. She hadn't said goodbye to the others either. Every time she thought about it, she got the urge to cry. Brayden had waved at her, excitement for his first storm on the ranch brimming in his eyes. Everyone else was too busy, and the last thing she wanted to do was interrupt them with a sappy goodbye and all the explanations that went along with it. Cole would have to explain it to them instead. Or he'd ignore their questions until they stopped asking.

She squeezed her eyes shut, straining to hear his truck coming down the road or his boots stomping on the back porch, but all she heard was the hammering of the rain on the tin roof, drowning out the whimper that escaped her.

Glancing at the clock, she knew she had waited long enough. She hoped he would come dashing in, begging her not to leave, but she had to admit that wasn't going to happen. The last kernel of hope sputtered out, leaving her bleak and empty.

She fought back tears as she laid the blanket on the back of the couch. Resting her hand on it, she sighed. Dropping an envelope on the counter, her vision blurring. At the door, she looked around one last time, at the place that had become more of a home to her in six months than her house in the city had in five years. Silently she said goodbye and walked out of Sundown Ranch forever.

Chapter Twenty-Six
Cole

THE storm made his job almost impossible, but at least it took all his focus and left little room to wonder if Abigail had left yet. Pretending nothing was wrong was easier. The ache in his chest was back though, steadily increasing as the day went on. He ignored it, along with everything else other than dealing with the storm.

He didn't even have time if he wanted to go after Abigail. They moved the cattle in the lower field to higher ground, but the fence got washed away. In a panic, the herd had moved back, trapping them, with the rising floodwaters almost surrounding them.

Cole was trying to yell to Diego on the other side, to get him to push them on towards the shelter, but he couldn't hear Cole over the downpour. He could faintly see the outline of his foreman's form, riding back and forth, trying to get them to move. Cows were hard enough to get to go where they wanted, but panicked cattle were almost impossible.

It took two hours, but they were able to get the herd out of danger for now. If the rain stopped tonight, the water wouldn't rise enough to reach the shelter. Diego was finishing up a headcount while Cole checked on the fencing around the building. The last thing he needed was them getting out again.

"We've got a problem, Cole."

Shit.

"What is it?"

"One's missing."

Cole sighed. Losing a cow was never what he wanted, but it happened. Especially during these squalls.

"Well, you'll have that," Cole said, looking over the herd.

"You don't get it Boss, it's Annabelle."

"Dammit."

* * *

Cole had been out searching for an hour. He sent Diego to the other pasture, hoping Annabelle had stayed there, but he had a feeling she hadn't followed the herd. A small calf, a few days weaned, wouldn't go off on their own, but Cole felt in his gut she was looking for something, or someone.

He rode towards the fence line, trying to spot a darker shape in the darkening night. If Annabelle had wandered off, he thought she might have tried to get to the spot where Abigail often visited, the same place he had taken her on their first official date.

His heart beat faster in his chest. He couldn't think about what would happen if he didn't find her. Abigail would be devastated. *He* would be devastated. He didn't want Abigail to lose both Betsy and Annabelle. That was her cow. How could he ever face her, look her in the eye and tell her Annabelle was gone? Lost to the forces of mother nature.

The farther he rode the more frantic he got. Trigger was pulling at the reins, struggling through the deepening mud. Cole had pushed him hard the last few hours, and they were both bone tired. But the potential loss of Annabelle had shocked Cole into overdrive. He had to find her. But as he came up to the spot, it was empty.

Dammit.

He thought for sure this was where he would find her, but Annabelle was lost to the storm. He turned Trigger around, intent on riding the line again. If he had to take his horse back and come out on foot he would. He'd hunt all night in this goddamn storm if he had to.

As he wheeled Trigger around, he heard a weak cry over the pounding rain. He twisted around in the saddle, scanning the darkness. Again, the faint bellow of a calf in distress echoed over the rain. He tried to pull Trigger around, but the horses' legs were stuck in the mud. Cole swung out of the saddle, wrapped the reins around the pommel, and struggled his way towards what he was sure was Annabelle. His boots sucked down in the mud with each step and still, he slogged on.

There, on a slight rise was the calf. Relief crashed into Cole with a force that almost brought him to his knees. Tears fell from his eyes, hidden by the rain. He hurried as fast as he could towards her, falling to his knees at her side.

"Hey, girl. It's okay. I've got you." She couldn't understand him, but he couldn't stop the words from pouring out of him. He checked her over as she bleated at him wearily.

"You were trying to get to her, weren't you? Don't worry girl. I'll get you out of here. I'll get you back to Abigail."

The relief at finding Annabelle was a balm to his soul. Cole rested his head on the calf's side, gathering comfort from the animal. He thought he had lost her. He expected the ache in his chest to lessen as the adrenaline eased, but it remained.

It hit him then he couldn't get the calf back to Abigail,

because she was gone. She'd never know Annabelle was lost, that he found her, brought her home. Abigail was gone. He hadn't fought for her. He hadn't tried. He hadn't thought he could. But now that he'd found Abigail's calf, he understood what Zach was talking about. This was fighting for her. He hadn't hesitated to ride out in this tempest to find Annabelle, because he couldn't bear the hurt it would cause the woman he loved. He'd found Annabelle but lost Abigail. He needed to get the calf back to safety, and find a way to fix things.

Not seeing anything physically wrong, other than exhaustion, he tried to heft the calf up, but she was a lot bigger now. After what felt like forever, she pulled her legs from under her and followed Cole back through the mud. He wanted to rush, to hurry back to the house and stop Abigail from leaving. He didn't entertain the possibility she was gone already, hoping the storm had done something productive and kept her safely on the ranch. He had to tell her he couldn't live without her because it would be a bleak wasteland without her like Zach said.

It took another hour to get back to the barn. He could have dropped Annabelle at the shelter, but he didn't want to take any chances, and besides, it was closer to the house. He sent one of the senior ranch hands to ride out and get Diego and ran to the house. It was still pouring down rain, forming rivers of water to break up the path in front of him.

He pounded up the steps of the porch, bursting through the French doors, but all the lights in the house were off. There were no signs of life as if Abigail took it all with her when she left. Mindlessly tracking mud across the floor, flipping on a light, he scanned the empty space and his eyes fell on the kitchen island. An envelope sat there, his name on the front in Abigail's writing. He wiped his hands and picked it up. It was thick, the flap hanging open, and he slipped the papers out and unfolded them, seeing the seal for Waterson & Avery printed on top.

A note fluttered to the counter, but his eyes were fixed, reading the paperwork that handed him the deed to the entire ranch. In a daze he set them down and picked up the note, reading it twice before the words sunk in. She had signed the ranch over to him. She added a condition of her own though. No payment other than the housing and care for Annabelle for the duration of her life. And he'd almost lost the calf, just like he was losing Abigail.

There was a crack of thunder, jolting him out of his daze. He rushed out the front door, intent on getting her back if he had to get on his knees and beg. It took twice for his truck to turn over. He wanted to speed down the drive, but it was an obstacle course of mud holes, bogging down his tires. He'd drive all the way to the city if he had to. No amount of distance was too far to go for her. He hoped she would forgive him when he finally caught up with her.

Chapter Twenty-Seven
Abby

THE drive back to the city took twice as long as it had six months ago. She thought she left early enough to beat the worst of the storm, but the rain wouldn't let up. Abby pulled into the drive, nostalgia overcoming her. Her house was dark, empty, and she felt it in her bones. Exhaustion was riding her hard, and it took everything in her to get out of the truck. Climbing the stairs, and ducking under the covered porch, she tried to keep her eyes on her own door, instead of looking for Muriel. She wouldn't be there. The sorrow was still there, buried under layers of pain Cole left in his wake.

Abby almost made it, but at the last second, she glanced over. Muriel's front porch had a swing on it now, the windows glowed with soft light, even with the rain. As she watched, a figure swept by the front window, a silhouette carrying a small child. A sob caught in her throat, seeing the father, dancing around Muriel's kitchen with his little one. Grief warred with awe inside her heart. Muriel may not be there, but the house was collecting more memories in her wake.

While Abby was at Sundown, the world moved on without her. She was in a bubble there, so caught up in the rollercoaster of her feelings for Cole, learning a new way of life, she almost forgot the rest of the world even existed. Sundown, Cole, became her world, and she would have been content living in that bubble the rest of her days. She knew that, regardless of what Cole said. Muriel gave Abby exactly what she needed, one more time. The anguish of having to leave it all behind, felt like losing Muriel all over again.

Unlocking her door, a musty scent hit her as disuse and dust tickled her nose. Abby rubbed her nose, holding back a sneeze. Her eyes were already filled with tears, and she didn't want them to fall. She'd cried enough over the loss of the life she left behind when she drove out of Sun Oak. She needed to pull herself together, find a way to say goodbye, because she couldn't fall in to the rote routine she was in when her parents died. She didn't know how she would pull herself out of it without Muriel if she did.

Abby flipped on the light, peering around the space that

had once been so familiar, but now was a void in her mind. It felt exactly like when she stepped into her childhood home to pack up her things after the car accident. At one point it was home, but it wasn't any longer. She gripped the door frame, to keep from collapsing. When she had control once more, she stepped in, not bothering to remove her shoes. There was so much dust on everything anyways she'd have to clean the floors regardless. Her favorite things were missing, still packed away in the truck. She turned on more lights as she went, every single one of them, trying to infuse the space with something, anything, but it didn't help. The emptiness remained. Setting her purse down on the kitchen counter, it tipped, spilling the contents on the floor.

"Dammit. Can't anything go right?" she sighed. Abby reached down to shove it all back in, but stalled, staring at the blue ribbon Annabelle won. She slid down, grasping it in her hands, fixating on the silken pin, contemplating what would happen to the calf now. Cole said she was Abby's, but now that she was gone…would he break his promise despite what she had done? A spear of anger spiked through her, wondering how he could do this to her, to them. She had half a mind to go back and tell him exactly what she thought of him, and what he'd done. She took responsibility for her role, but he couldn't do the same.

As quickly as the fury grabbed her, it flowed away,

replaced by the empty ache that was her constant companion since Cole told her things were better this way. It wasn't better. Nothing was better. This house, this city, it was empty. She was empty. Abby didn't belong here anymore. She knew it before, but seeing the place again only solidified it was no longer her home.

Shoving the random items back in her bag, Abby bolted out the front door, barely stopping to lock it. No matter what, she had to try, one last time. If Cole wouldn't listen, if he really was done with her, so be it. She wouldn't let him run her out of town though. Her soul belonged in Sun Oak. She knew it belonged on the ranch, but if Cole wouldn't listen…she shoved the thought away. She was done hiding. She was done making herself small. She was done being ashamed and apologizing for being who she was. Abby wasn't a city girl, and she was done trying to fit that mold. Her soul lived in the fields, in the land, in the work, and she wasn't going to give that up.

The rain picked up more, if that was possible. No other cars were on the road, which helped, since Abby was pretty sure she wasn't on her side of the road most of the time, especially when the buildings and lights faded away, leaving the night darker than she'd seen it since she'd moved in May. She kept her eyes glued to the road, which left little room for the thoughts of what she'd do when she finally got back to

Sundown to intrude. Abby almost missed the driveway and slammed on the brakes, making the tires skid, even though she was crawling along.

She made the turn slowly, navigating the muddy trail that constituted a driveway out here. Her knuckles were white on the steering wheel, while her mind raced, trying to decide if she wanted to cuss Cole out or beg him to give them another chance.

Her truck slid around a curve, and she cranked the wheel, trying to straighten out. But the entire thing jerked to a stop, whipping her forward and locking the seat belt, saving her head from hitting the steering wheel. Abby pushed the gas, but the tires spun aimlessly, spitting mud up on the windshield, blocking her view as the rain made tracks through the mess. She unbuckled to stop the belt from strangling her.

It was too much. Between leaving the note for Cole, choosing to walk away from what she was sure was the only life she was meant to live, from the only man she'd ever loved, then seeing her house and deciding to try one last time, she broke. Her heart shattered in her chest, and she screamed as the tears she held back all day flowed down her face. Abby beat at the steering wheel, wailing against the world, and at the cruel circumstances that brought her to this exact moment. All she wanted was feel Cole's arms around her, telling her everything would be okay. The fact that it might never happen was too much. She laid her head on the wheel and tears flowed down her face.

A knock at her window made her jerk up. Standing in the rain, covered in mud, was Cole. She covertly tried to wipe her eyes on her sleeve, but he yanked the door open before she could hide the evidence.

"What the hell are you doing, driving in this weather?" he demanded, as if he had the right to yell at her. She couldn't speak, stunned he was here. She hadn't expected to see him out here. She thought she'd have more time to figure out what to say.

"Seriously Abigail, you could have killed yourself!" She could feel his eyes scanning her face, but it wasn't anger, it was concern shining out of them.

"I'm sorry," she said feebly, not knowing what else to say. She didn't know what she was apologizing for anymore. There were so many things she looked back on and wished went differently.

"Don't be sorry, tell me what the hell you were thinking."

Staring at him, she didn't know how to answer. Everything they went through, worked through, wasn't enough. The terms of the will were over. She'd signed over the ranch. She'd let go of the possibility of having the future Abby thought she'd have with him, in this place where she'd found home. Now that he was here, it seemed silly to come back, to try to talk some sense into him. What could she possibly say that would change his mind? Nothing. The emptiness she'd felt walking into her place in the city welled up in her chest, threatening to choke off her breath.

Abby let out a gust of breath, looking away, "I'm thinking this is done."

"Do you want it done?"

"What does it matter Cole?! You gave up. You didn't want to fight for this, for us. You'd rather stay stuck. Stuck at this ranch alone, stuck in your rut, existing and never wanting more, wanting me. You didn't want me to stay, but now when I left you think you can come in and yell at me?" The fury and sorrow blended together, forcing the words out as the tears came back, soaking her face and mixing with the rain that was finally easing up.

"I know. I know I messed up Abigail. You were right."

She glanced at him, the anger seeping out of her. His face fell, dark eyes holding regret and the hint of something else; something she couldn't name.

"I don't know what to say to that."

"You don't have to say anything. Just listen. I thought I was doing the right thing. I thought letting you go was better for you, but I was lying to myself. You were right. I built those walls, thinking it was better this way. I convinced myself I was never going to find someone who loved this place as much as I did, but then you came along and you fit right in, you came alive here, your soul is here as much as mine is. I never thought I'd find that, and then I pushed you away because I was scared. I want to spend every day showing you how much I love you instead of regretting I never told you. The only thing I need to know is what you want, what you really want."

"I can't keep doing this Cole. What happens the next time something comes along? The next time something goes wrong? What happens then?" Abby demanded.

"I don't know. I want to tell you it won't happen, that it'll be different, and I'll sure as hell try, Honey, but I can't promise you I won't mess up. But I will never walk away from you again. I need you here. Muriel knew that. It's why she gave you all she did in her will, and she gave me the chance with you. I'm sorry I messed it up."

"I don't own the ranch anymore, Cole. I gave it to you! You don't owe me anything." Abby's heart flipped in her chest as she tucked her head. Had he missed the paperwork she'd left? She left it where she was sure he wouldn't miss it, but maybe he hadn't been back to the house yet.

"This paperwork?" he asked, pulling the paperwork out of his back pocket, rain splattering on the pages. "It's not worth it if I don't have you, Abigail."

Abby's mouth fell open as he ripped it up, dropping the papers in the mud, eyes fixed on her.

"Honey, tell me what I have to do. I'll do anything if you just give me a chance. One more chance to prove to you how much I love you, how much I want you to stay. Please," Cole begged, while the rain misted around his shoulders.

"I want to stay," Abby gasped out, relief and hope bursting inside her.

Swiftly, she was yanked out of the car and into Cole's arms. He wrapped them around her, holding her close. His head ducked near her ear, and he said what she felt she'd been waiting for her whole life.

"You sure you want to be stuck here with me?"

Abby tried to pull back, to see into his face, but his arms tightened around her. Her voice, muffled by his wet shirt, came out in a puff, "I'd be stuck anywhere as long as I can be with you, but especially if it's here. I love you."

Cole's lips met hers. They stood for a long time, holding each other as the rain fell around them softly. Finally, finding where they belonged.

The End

Thank you so much for reading Cole and Abigail's story!

They've lived in my head for so long, I'm happy to be able to share them with you now.

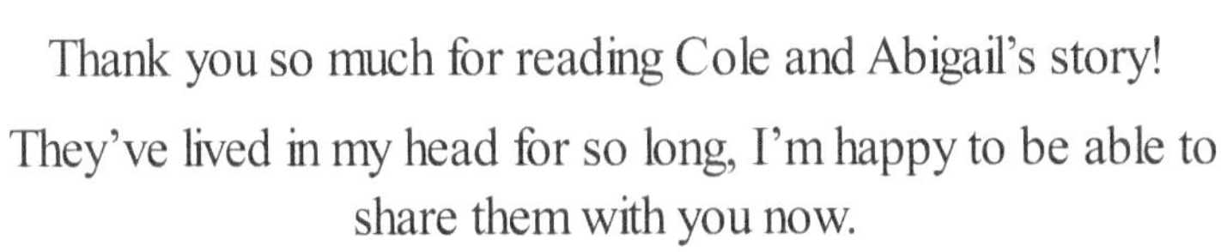

If you'd like to hear about the other stories that have been living in my head, sign up for my newsletter, visit my website, or follow me on social media visit

emiliaabraham.com

About the Author

After many years of dreaming of becoming a full-time writer, Emilia Abraham took the leap, bringing her words to print. From sweet contemporary romance to spicy reverse harem and everything in between, she focuses on the happily ever after.

Emilia lives in the Upper Midwest with her husband (who's probably sick of listening to her expound on fictional men) and three kids (who try to steal her post-it notes). When she's not writing, she enjoys reading, playing video games, and consuming copious amounts of energy drinks.